"I want to kiss you." Lukas couldn't stop the words, only knew them for the truth they were. "You know that, don't you?"

Holly's cheeks went red, and she shook her head rapidly. "No!" She took a quick breath. "Not a good idea."

"Why not?"

"Because...because I said not." She wouldn't look at him.

"Afraid I won't follow through?" Lukas pressed. "Or that I will?"

She jerked away from him. "Stop it!" She crossed the room, put the desk between them.

"There's something between us," he told her. "Don't tell me you don't feel it."

OCT 1 5

Bestselling two-time RITA® Award winner (with a further nine finalist titles) **Anne McAllister** has written nearly seventy books for Harlequin Presents, American Romance, Desire, Special Edition and single titles, which means she basically follows the characters no matter where they take her. She loves to travel, but at home she and her husband divide their time between Montana and Iowa. Anne loves to hear from readers. Contact her at annemcallister.com.

Books by Anne McAllister

Harlequin Presents

Breaking the Greek's Rules
Hired by Her Husband
The Virgin's Proposition
One-Night Mistress...Convenient Wife

Return of the Rebels

Savas's Wildcat

Tall, Dark and Dangerously Sexy

The Night that Changed Everything

Greek Tycoons

The Santorini Bride
Antonides' Forbidden Wife

In Bed with the Boss

The Boss's Wife for a Week

Visit the Author Profile page
at Harlequin.com for more titles.

Anne McAllister

—

The Return of Antonides

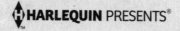

HARLEQUIN PRESENTS®

ISBN-13: 978-0-373-13381-9

The Return of Antonides

First North American Publication 2015

Copyright © 2015 by Barbara Schenck

The publisher acknowledges the copyright holder
of the additional work:

Christmas at the Castello
Copyright © 2015 by Amanda Cinelli

Recycling programs
for this product may
not exist in your area.

Printed in U.S.A.

The Return of Antonides

For Anne

CHAPTER ONE

"GETTING MARRIED IS EXHAUSTING." Althea Halloran Rivera Smith Moore collapsed into the back of the cab and closed her eyes, unmoving.

"Which is why you're only supposed to do it once," Holly said drily as she clambered in after her sister-in-law. She pulled the door shut and gave the driver her address in Brooklyn.

As the taxi edged back out into the late Saturday afternoon Midtown Manhattan traffic, Holly slumped back in against the seat. "Those dresses were horrible." She shuddered just thinking about the pastel creations she'd tried on all day. It wasn't as if she hadn't worn identically repulsive bridesmaids' dresses for Althea's other weddings.

"This is the last time." Althea put her hand over her heart. "I swear. I'm just too impulsive."

In the eight years since Holly's wedding to Althea's brother Matt, Althea had marched up the aisle three times. And into divorce court each time shortly thereafter.

"But not anymore. This time is different," Althea assured her. "Stig is different."

Swedish professional hockey player Stig Mikkelsen had nothing at all in common with the aloof doctor, the extroverted stock broker and the pompous professor Althea had married previously. Stig had swept into Althea's life six months ago, charmed her, teased her and refused to take no for an answer. He'd overturned her resolve never to walk down another aisle, and best of all, had somehow given Althea the greatest gift—helping her return to the sparkling, cheerful woman she had been before her three marital disasters.

For that alone, Holly blessed him. So when Althea began making wedding plans and asked Holly to be her "one and only bridesmaid, please, please, please!" Holly had gritted her teeth and agreed.

She'd even silently vowed—if necessary—to force herself into another stiff, ruffled, pastel cupcake of a dress. But even with just the two of them to please and all of Manhattan's gauziest wonders to choose from, they hadn't been able to find "the perfect bridesmaid's dress."

"Stig will know what we need. I'll take him next time," Althea said.

"He's a nice guy," Holly allowed. But if he went dress shopping with Althea, he should be nominated for sainthood.

"And he's got teammates…" Althea shot her a speculative look. "Single ones."

"No," Holly said automatically. "Not interested." She crossed her arms over her tote bag, holding it against her like a shield.

"You don't even know what I was going to say!"

Holly arched a brow. "Don't I?"

Althea had the grace to look a tiny bit abashed, then gave a little flounce and lifted her chin. "Some of them are very nice guys."

"No doubt. I'm not interested."

"You're not even thirty years old! You have a whole life ahead of you!"

"I know." There was nothing Holly was more aware of

than how much of her life there still might be—and how flat and empty it was. She pressed her lips together and made herself stare at the cars they were passing.

Suddenly Althea's hand was on her knee, giving it a sympathetic squeeze. "I know you miss him," she said, her voice soft but thick with emotion. "We all miss him."

Matt, she meant. Her brother. Holly's husband. The center of Holly's life.

Just thirty years old, Matthew David Halloran had had everything to live for. He was bright, witty, handsome, charming. A psychologist who worked mostly with children and teens, Matt had loved his work. He'd loved life.

He had loved hiking, skiing and camping. He'd loved astronomy and telescopes, basketball and hockey. He'd loved living in New York City, loved the fifth floor walkup he and Holly had shared when they'd first moved to the city, loved the view across the river to Manhattan from the condo they'd recently bought in a trendy Brooklyn high-rise.

Most of all, Matt had loved his wife.

He'd told her so that Saturday morning two years and four months ago. He had bent down and kissed her sleepy smile as he'd gone out the door to play basketball with his buddies. "Love you, Hol'," he'd murmured.

Holly had reached up from the bed she was still snuggled in and snagged his hand and kissed it. "You could show me," she'd suggested with a sleepy smile.

Matt had given her a rueful grin. "Temptress." Then he'd winked. "I'll be home at noon. Hold that thought."

It was the last thing he'd ever said to her. Two hours later Matt Halloran was dead. An aneurysm, they told her later. Unknown and undetected. A silent killer waiting for the moment to strike.

Going in for a lay-up at the end of the game, Matt had shot—and dropped to the floor.

Simultaneously the bottom had dropped out of Holly's world.

At first she had been numb. Disbelieving. Not Matt. He couldn't be dead. He hadn't been sick. He was healthy as a horse. He was strong. Capable. He had his whole life ahead of him!

But it turned out that Holly was the one who had her life ahead of her—a life without Matt. A life she hadn't planned on.

It hadn't been easy. All she had wanted to do those first months was cry. She couldn't because she had a class full of worried fifth graders to teach. They looked to her for guidance. They knew Matt because he and Holly took them to the marina on Saturdays to teach them canoeing and kayaking. They shared her grief and needed a role model for how to handle it.

Psychologist Matt would have been the first to tell her so.

So for them, Holly had stopped wallowing in misery. She'd wiped away her tears, pasted on her best smile and resolutely put one foot in front of the other again.

Eventually, life began to resemble something akin to normal, though for her it never would be again—not without Matt to share it.

But even though she had learned to cope, she wasn't prepared when friends and family began trying to set her up with another man. Holly didn't *want* another man! She wanted the man she'd had.

But ever since last summer Althea had been dropping hints. Holly's brother, Greg, a lawyer in Boston, said he had a colleague she might like to meet. Even her mother, a longtime divorcee with not much good to say about men, had suggested she take a singles cruise. At Christmas Matt's parents had begun telling her she needed to get on with her life, that Matt would want her to.

She'd always done everything Matt wanted her to. That was the problem!

"At least you're dating Paul."

"Yes." A few months back, Holly had determined that the best way to deter meddling family and friends was to appear to have taken their advice and gone out. Charming, handsome, smart, a psychologist like Matt, Paul McDonald was *like* Matt. But he *wasn't* Matt. So no danger to her at all. It just kept well-meaning relatives and friends off her back. And she knew she wasn't leading Paul on. Long divorced, Paul was a complete cynic about marriage.

"If you married Paul," Althea said, oblivious to Paul's lack of interest, "you wouldn't have to hare off across the world to sit on a coral atoll somewhere." She gave Holly an indignant glare. "I can't believe you're even considering that!"

Joining the Peace Corps, she meant. Last fall, fed up with the emptiness of her life and admitting to herself at least that she needed to find a new purpose, a new focus, Holly had sent in her application. They had offered her a two-year teaching position on a small South Pacific island. She was to start preliminary training in Hawaii the second week in August.

"I'm not considering. I'm doing it," she said now.

"Paul can't talk you out of it?"

"No."

"Someone should," Althea grumbled. "You need a man who will make you sit up and take notice. Paul's too nice. You need a challenge." Abruptly, she sat up straight, a smile dawning on her lips. "Like Lukas Antonides."

"What? *Who?*" Holly felt as if all the air had been

sucked out of the universe. She was gasping as she stared at her sister-in-law. Where had *that* come from?

"You remember Lukas." Althea was practically bouncing on the seat now, her cheeks definitely rosy.

Holly felt hers burning. Her whole body was several degrees warmer. "I remember Lukas."

"You used to follow him around," Althea said.

"I did not! I followed Matt!" It was Matt, damn him, who had followed Lukas around.

Lukas Antonides had become the neighborhood equivalent of the Pied Piper from the minute he'd moved in the year he and Matt were eleven and Holly was nine.

"Ah, Lukas." Althea used her dreamy voice. "He was such a stud. He still is."

"How do you know?" Holly said dampeningly. "He's on the other side of the world."

Lukas had spent the past half dozen years or so in Australia. Before that he'd been in Europe—Greece, Sweden, France. Not that she'd kept track of him. Matt had done that.

Since Matt's death she hadn't really known where Lukas was. She'd received a sympathy card simply signed "Lukas." No personal remarks. Nothing—except the spiky black scrawl of his name—which was absolutely fine with her.

She hadn't expected him at the funeral. It was too far to come. And thank God for that. She hadn't had to deal with him along with everything else. For a dozen years now she hadn't had to deal with him at all. So why was Althea bringing him up now, when he was off mining opals or wrangling kangaroos or doing whatever enthusiasm was grabbing him at the moment?

"He's back," Althea said. "Didn't you see the article in *What's New!*?"

Holly felt her stomach clench. "No." It was the end of the school year. She didn't have time to read anything except student papers. "What article?" *What's New!* was a hot, upscale lifestyle magazine. Out of her league. She wouldn't normally read it anyway.

Since getting engaged to Stig, Althea always read it. Sometimes she was even in it. Now she nodded eagerly. "Gorgeous article. Just like him." She grinned. "He got the centerfold."

"They don't have centerfolds in *What's New!*" But the image it conjured up made Holly's cheeks flame.

Althea laughed. "The centerfold of the magazine. There's a double-page spread of Lukas in his office. Big story about him and his foundation and the gallery he's opening."

"Foundation? Gallery? What gallery?"

"He's opening a gallery for Australian, New Zealand and Pacific art here in New York. Big stuff in the local art community. And he's heading up some charitable foundation."

"Lukas?" If the gallery and the centerfold boggled her mind, the notion of Lukas heading up a charitable foundation sounded like a sign of the apocalypse.

"It's in this week's issue," Althea went on. "He's on the cover, too. Surprised it didn't catch your eye. The gallery is in SoHo. They showed some of the art and sculpture in the article. Very trendy. It's going to draw lots of interest." Her grin widened. "So is Lukas."

Holly folded her hands in her lap, staring straight ahead. "How nice."

Althea made a tutting sound. "What do you have against Lukas? You were friends."

"He was Matt's friend," Holly insisted.

Lukas's move into the neighborhood had turned Holly's

life upside down. Until then she and Matt had been best friends. But once Lukas arrived, she'd been relegated to tag-along, particularly by Lukas.

Matt hadn't ditched her completely. Solid, dependable, responsible Matt had always insisted that Holly was his friend. But when Lukas's father took them out in his sailboat, she hadn't been invited.

"Go play with Martha," Lukas had said. It had been his answer to everything.

His twin sister, Martha, had spent hours drawing and sketching everything in sight. Holly couldn't draw a stick figure without a ruler. She'd liked swimming and playing ball and catching frogs and riding bikes. She'd liked all the same things Matt did.

Except Lukas.

If Matt had always been as comfortable as her oldest shoes, Lukas was like walking on nails. Dangerous. Unpredictable. Fascinating in the way that, say, Bengal tigers were fascinating. And perversely, she'd never been able to ignore him.

If Lukas was back, she had yet another reason to be glad she was leaving.

"He's made a fortune opal mining, apparently," Althea told her. "And he's parlayed it into successful businesses across the world. He's got fingers in lots of pies, your Lukas."

"He's not *my* Lukas," Holly said, unable to stop herself.

"Well, you should consider him," Althea said, apparently seriously. "He's handsomer than ever. Animal magnetism and all that." Althea flapped a hand like a fan in front of her face. "Seriously hot."

"Hotter than Stig?"

"No one's hotter than Stig," Althea said with a grin. "But Lukas is definitely loaded with sex appeal."

"And knows it, too, I'm sure," Holly said. He always had. Once he'd noticed the opposite sex, Lukas had gone through women like a shark went through minnows.

"Well, you should look him up—for old times' sake," Althea said firmly.

"I don't think so." Holly cast about for a change in subject, then realized happily that she didn't need to. The taxi had just turned onto her street.

Althea shrugged. "Suit yourself. But I'd pick him over Paul any day of the week."

"Be my guest." Holly gathered up her sweater and tote bag.

"Nope. I've got my man." Althea gave a smug, satisfied smile.

Once I had mine, too, Holly thought. She didn't say it. There was no reason to make Althea feel guilty because she had found the love of her life and Holly had lost hers. "Hang on to him," she advised, getting out her share of the taxi fare.

"Put that away. The taxi is on me. I'm sorry we didn't find a dress. Maybe next Saturday…"

"Can't. I'm going to be kayaking with the kids from school next Saturday." She'd only missed going today because Althea had begged her.

"Then maybe I'll take Stig. Do you trust me to do it on my own?"

Trust her? After Althea had dressed her like a cupcake with too much frosting three times before?

Wincing inwardly, Holly pasted on her best resilient-bridesmaid smile. "Of course I trust you. It's your wedding. I'll wear whatever you choose."

Althea gave Holly a fierce hug. "You're such a trouper, Hol', hanging in with me through all my weddings." She pulled back and looked at Holly with eyes the same flecked hazel as Matt's. "I know it's been tough. I know it's been an awful two years. I know life will never be the same. It won't be for any of us. But Matt would want you to be happy again. You know he would."

Holly's throat tightened and her eyes blurred, because yes, she knew Matt would want that, damn him. Matt had never focused on the downside. Whenever life had dealt him lemons or a broken leg—though it had actually been Lukas who'd dealt him that, she recalled—Matt had coped. He would expect her to do the same.

"The right guy will come along," Althea assured Holly as she opened the cab door. "I know he will. Just like Stig did for me when I'd given up all hope."

"Sure," Holly humored her as she stepped out onto the curb and turned back to smile.

Althea grinned. "You never know. It might even be Lukas."

Lukas Antonides used to feel at home in New York City. He used to be in tune with its speed, its noise, its color, its pace of life. Once upon a time he'd got energized by it. Now all he got was a headache.

Or maybe it wasn't the city giving him a headache. Maybe it was the rest of his life.

Lukas thrived on hard work and taking charge. But he had always known that if he wanted to, he could simply pick up and walk away. He couldn't walk away from the gallery—didn't want to. But being everything to every artist and craftsperson who was counting on him—and the gallery—when for years he had resisted being responsible for anyone other than himself made his head pound.

Ordinarily, he loved hard physical labor. Throwing himself body and soul into whatever he was doing gave him energy. That was why he'd taken over the renovation of not only the gallery, but the rest of the offices and apartments in the cast-iron SoHo building he'd bought three months ago. But the gallery cut into the time he had for that, and getting behind where he thought he should be was causing a throb behind his eyes.

And then there was his mother who, since he'd got back from Australia, had been saying not so sotto voce, "Is she the one?" whenever he mentioned a woman's name. He knew she was angling for another daughter-in-law. It was what Greek mothers did. He'd been spared before as there were other siblings to pressure. But they were all married now, busily providing the next generation.

Only he was still single.

"I'll marry when I'm ready," he'd told her flatly. He didn't tell her that he didn't see it happening. He'd long ago missed that boat.

But more than anything, he was sure the headache—the pounding behind his eyes, the throbbing that wouldn't go away—was caused by the damned stalagmites of applications for grants by the MacClintock Foundation, which, for his sins, he was in charge of.

"Just a few more," his secretary, Serafina, announced with dry irony, dropping another six-inch stack onto his desk.

Lukas groaned and pinched the bridge of his nose. The headache spiked. He wasn't cut out for this sort of thing. He was an action man, not a paper-pusher. And Skeet MacClintock had known that!

But it hadn't stopped the late Alexander "Skeet" MacClintock, Lukas's cranky friend and opal-mining mentor, from guilting him into taking on the job of running the foundation and vetting the applicants. He'd known that Lukas wouldn't be able to turn his back on Skeet's plan for a foundation intended to "Give a guy—or gal—a hand. Or a push."

Because once Skeet had given Lukas a hand. And this, damn it, was his way of pushing.

Lukas sighed and gave Sera a thin smile. "Thanks."

"There are more," Sera began.

"Spare me."

Sera smiled. "You'll get there."

Lukas grunted. For all that he'd rather be anywhere else, he owed this to Skeet.

The old man, an ex-pat New Yorker like himself, had provided the grumbling, cantankerous steadiness that a young, hotheaded, quicksilver Lukas had needed six years ago. Not that Lukas had known it at the time.

He would have said they were just sharing digs in a dusty, blisteringly hot or perversely cold mining area in the outback. Skeet could have tossed him out. Lukas could have left at any time.

Often he had, taking jobs crewing on schooners or yachts. He'd leave for months, never promising to come back, never intending to. But for all his wanderlust and his tendency to jump from one thing to next, there was something about opal mining—about the possibilities and the sheer hard work—that energized him and simultaneously took the edge off his restlessness. For the first time in years, he had slept well at night.

He felt good. He and Skeet got along. Skeet never made any demands. Not even when he got sick. He just soldiered on. And at the end, he had only one request.

"Makin' you my executor," he'd rasped at Lukas during the last few days. "You take care of things…after."

Lukas had wanted to deny furiously that there would be an "after," that Skeet MacClintock would die and the world would go on. But Skeet was a realist. "Whaddya say?" Skeet's faded blue eyes had bored into Lukas's own.

By that time the old man had seemed more like a father to him than his own. Of course Lukas had said yes. How hard would it be? He'd only have to distribute the old man's assets.

Skeet had plenty, though no one would ever have guessed from the Spartan underground digs he called home. Lukas only knew of Skeet's business acumen because Skeet had helped him parlay his own mining assets into a considerable fortune.

Even so, he had never imagined the old man had a whole foundation up his sleeve—one offering monetary grants to New Yorkers who needed "someone to believe in them so they could dare to believe in themselves."

Who'd have thought Skeet would have such a sentimental streak? Not Lukas. Though he should have expected there would be a stampede of New Yorkers eager to take advantage of it when the news spread.

He'd had a trickle of applications before the *What's New!* article. But once it hit the stands, the postman began staggering in with bags and bags of mail.

That was when Serafina had proved her worth. A fiftysomething, no-nonsense mother of seven, Serafina Delgado could organize a battalion, deal with flaky artists and cantankerous sculptors and prioritize grant applications, all while answering the phone and keeping a smile on her face. Lukas, who didn't multitask worth a damn, was impressed.

"Sort 'em out," he'd instructed her. "Only give me the ones you think I really ought to consider."

He would make the final decisions himself. Skeet's instructions had been clear about that.

"How the hell will I know who needs support?" Lukas had demanded.

"You'll know." Skeet had grinned faintly from his hospital bed. "They'll be the ones that remind you of me."

That was why the old man had created the foundation in the first place, and Lukas knew it. Back when it mattered, when he was in his twenties, Skeet hadn't believed in himself. Deeply in love with a wealthy young New York socialite, poor boy Skeet hadn't felt he had anything to offer her besides his love. So he'd never dared propose.

"Didn't believe enough in myself," he had told Lukas one cold day last winter, fossicking through rubble for opals.

They didn't have heart-to-hearts, never talked about much personal stuff at all. Only mining. Football. Beer. Skeet's sudden veer in a personal direction should have warned Lukas things were changing.

"Don't pay to doubt yourself," Skeet had gone on. And Lukas learned that by the time Skeet had made something of himself and had gone back to pop the question, Millicent had married someone else.

"So, what? You want me to play matchmaker to New York City?" Lukas hadn't been able to decide whether he was amused or appalled.

Skeet chuckled. "Not necessarily. But most folks got somethin' they want to reach for and don't quite got the guts to do." He'd met Lukas's gaze levelly. "Reckon you know that."

Then it had been Lukas's turn to look away. He'd never said, but he knew Skeet had seen through his indifferent dismissal to a past that Lukas had never really confronted once he'd walked away.

Now, determinedly, he shoved all the memories away again and forced himself to go back to reading the applications. It was the first week of June. The deadline for application submissions was two weeks away. Now he had thousands of them. Even with Sera sorting through them, he needed to read faster.

He stared at the paper in front of him until his eyes crossed…then shut…

"Grace called."

Lukas's head jerked up. "What?"

Sera stood in the doorway frowning at him. "She says to pick her up at her grandmother's at a quarter to eight. Were you sleeping?"

"No. Of course not." Though from the hands on the clock above the file cabinet he'd been closing his eyes for over half an hour. Now he tried not to let his jaw crack with a yawn. He'd winced, realizing he had forgotten all about Grace. She was Millicent's granddaughter, and Lukas sometimes wondered if she were Skeet's own attempt at matchmaking from beyond the grave. The old man had found out a bit about Millicent's life over the years. Chances were he'd known about Grace. He raked a hand through his hair. "Why didn't you put her through?"

"She said not to bother, to just give you the message." Sera studied him narrowly. "Are you all right?"

"I'm fine." Lukas stifled another yawn. "Just bored."

"Go meet Grace then," Sera suggested with a grin. "You won't be bored."

"Can't. Got to finish this." He glanced at his watch. "Time for you to go home, though."

"Soon. I have a few more applications to go through. You can do this," she said briskly in her den-mother voice. Then she shut the door behind her.

Lukas stood and stretched, then paced the room, trying to muster some enthusiasm for dinner with Grace. He shouldn't have to muster enthusiasm at all.

Grace was wonderful. His mother liked Grace. Sera liked Grace. Everyone liked Grace. Grace Marchand spoke five languages, had degrees in art history and museum conservation. She coordinated special exhibits for one of the city's major art museums. She was blonde and blue-eyed and beautiful, looking a lot like her grandmother must have half a century ago. Skeet would have loved her.

Because of that, Lukas had taken her out several times since—to dinner, to a concert, some charity functions, a couple of command-performance family dinners. Grace was good company. She knew which fork to use, which was more than he often did. In his new more social role, he was grateful for that. But regardless of what Skeet might have been plotting or Lukas's mother might be hoping, he wasn't marrying her.

And now he really had come full circle because his head was throbbing again.

The door from the outer office opened once more, and Sera came in.

"I thought you were leaving?" Lukas said sharply.

Sera nodded. "On my way. Just finished the applications. There's one that you should see." She waved the envelope in her hand.

"I don't want to see another application tonight." He held out a hand to ward her off. "I've had it up to my eyeballs. Every person in New York City wants me to give them half a million dollars."

"Not this lady." Sera waved the envelope again. "She only wants half a boat!"

Lukas felt the words like a punch in the gut. "Half a—? *What?*"

Sera shrugged, grinning as she set the papers on his desk. "Half a boat. Can you believe it?"

Lukas crossed the room in three long strides and snatched up the papers from the desk. There was only one woman in the world who would ask him for half a boat—Holly.

Holly. After all these years. Lukas wasn't bored anymore. His heart was pounding even as he stared at her signature at the bottom of a typed business letter on ivory paper.

Holly Montgomery Halloran. Firm, spiky, no-nonsense letters—just like the woman who had written them. He exhaled sharply just looking at her name. The letter had a letterhead from St. Brendan's School, Brooklyn, New York. Where she taught. Matt had told him that a few years back. The letter was brief, but he didn't have a chance to read it because with it, fluttering out of the envelope, came a photograph of a sailboat.

Lukas snatched it out of the air before it hit the floor and, staring at it, felt a mixture of pain and longing and loss as big as a rock-size gouge that there had been in the hull when he had last seen the boat in person. Someone— Matt—had repaired the hull. But the mast was still broken. Snapped right off, the way he remembered it. And there was still plenty of rotten wood. The boat needed work. A lot of work.

Lukas felt a tingle at the back of his neck and faint buzzing inside his head. He dropped into his chair and realized he wasn't breathing.

"Yours?" Sera queried.

"Half." Lukas dragged the word up from the depth of his being. It sounded rusty, as if he hadn't said it in years.

Sera smiled. "Which half?"

There was no answer to that. He shook his head.

"I thought you must know her," Sera said gently. "Holly?" Because, of course, Sera had read the letter.

"Yes."

Sera waited, but when he didn't say more, she nodded. "Right. Well, then," she said more briskly. "Well, you deal with Holly and the boat. I'm off."

Lukas didn't look up. He waited until he heard the door shut. Then he picked up the letter, not seeing anything but the signature. Then he shut his eyes.

He didn't need them to see Holly as clear as day.

He had a kaleidoscope of memories to choose from: Holly at nine, all elbows and skinned knees and attitude; Holly at thirteen, still coltish but suddenly curvy, running down the beach; Holly at fifteen, her swingy dark hair with auburn highlights, loose and luxuriant, her breasts a handful; Holly at seventeen, blue eyes soft with love as she'd looked adoringly at Matt; Holly at eighteen, blue eyes hard, accusing Lukas when Matt had broken his leg; and then, two weeks later, Holly on the night of her senior prom—beautiful and nervy, edgy and defiant. Then gentler, softer, laughing, smiling—at him for once.

And then Holly in the night, on his father's boat, her eyes doubtful, then apprehensive, then wondering, and finally—

Lukas made a strangled sound deep in his throat.

He dropped the photo on the desk and, with unsteady fingers, picked up the letter—to read the first words he'd had from Holly Halloran in a dozen years.

CHAPTER TWO

WHERE THE HELL was she?

Lukas stood on the marina dock, hands on hips, squinting as he scanned the water, trying to pick Holly out of the Saturday-morning crowd of canoes and kayaks and pedal boats that were maneuvering in a sheltered basin on the banks of the Brooklyn side of the East River.

He should have been hanging drywall in one of the lofts above the gallery or helping set up the display cases in one of the artisans' workshops. He should have, God save him, been reading more of the apparently endless supply of MacClintock grant applications.

Instead, he was here.

Because Holly was here.

Or so the principal of St. Brendan's School had promised him.

Three days ago, as he'd read her stilted, determinedly impersonal letter requesting that he join her in making a gift to St. Brendan's School of the sailboat he and Matt had intended to restore while they were in college, because she was "tying up loose ends before she left," a tidal wave of long-suppressed memories and emotions had washed over him.

He could, of course, keep right on suppressing them. He'd had plenty of practice. So for all of thirty-six hours he'd tried to push Holly back in the box he'd deliberately shut a dozen years ago.

It was over, he'd told himself, which wasn't quite the truth. The truth was, it had never really begun. And he should damned well leave it that way.

But he couldn't. He couldn't just sign the deed of gift she'd attached to the letter. He couldn't just walk away. Truth to tell, the mere thought of Holly was the first thing to really energize him since he'd come home.

So on impulse, he had called St. Brendan's and asked to speak to her.

Of course it had been the middle of the school day. Holly was teaching. The secretary offered to take a message.

Lukas said no. He could leave a message, but she wouldn't call him back. He knew Holly. If she had wanted to talk to him, she would have given him her number in the letter. She'd have written to him on her own notepaper, not printed out an impersonal little message on a St. Brendan's official letterhead.

He got the message: Holly still didn't want anything to do with him.

But it didn't mean she was going to get her way. He called back and spoke to the principal.

Father Morrison was pleasant and polite and had known instantly who Lukas was. "Matt spoke very highly of you."

"Matt?" That was a surprise.

"He volunteered here. He and Holly taught extracurricular kayaking and canoeing. Matt wanted to teach the kids to sail. Right before he died, he told me he had a boat they could use. After... Well, I didn't want to mention it to Holly. But she brought it up a few days ago, said she had written to you hoping you'd agree to make it a gift to the school." The statement had been as much question as explanation.

"I want to talk to Holly," Lukas said, deliberately not answering it. "I've just moved back from Australia. I don't have her phone number."

"And I can't give it to you. Privacy, you know," Father Morrison said apologetically. Then he added, "But you might run into her at the marina. She still goes there most Saturday mornings to teach the kids."

"I might do that," Lukas said. "Thanks, Father."

So here he was pacing the dock, still unable to spot her. He hadn't seen Holly since her wedding ten years ago. Every time he'd been back since—less than half a dozen times in the whole decade—he'd seen Matt, but never Holly.

She had been visiting her mother or at a bridal shower or taking books back to the library. Maybe it had been true. Certainly Matt seemed to think nothing of Holly's excuses. But Matt didn't know Holly was avoiding him.

Now Lukas jammed his hands into the pockets of his cargo shorts, annoyed that she was so hard to spot, more annoyed that he cared. His brain said there was no sense dusting things up after all this time. He probably wouldn't even recognize her.

He'd recognize her.

He knew it as sure as he knew his own name.

A day hadn't gone by that Holly hadn't wiggled her way into his consciousness. She had been a burr in his skin for years, an itch he had wanted to scratch since he'd barely known that such itches existed.

A couple of days after his family had moved from the city out to the far reaches of Long Island, he had met Matt. They had been standing under a tree near his house, and

Lukas had said his dad would take him and Matt sailing, that it would be cool to have a new best friend.

And suddenly a skinny, freckle-faced urchin dropped out of the tree between them and stuck her face in his. "You can't be Matt's best friend. I already am!" She'd kicked him in the shin. He'd pulled her braid. It had pretty much gone downhill from there.

Lukas had two sisters already. He didn't need another girl in his life, especially one who insisted on dogging his and Matt's footsteps day after day after day.

"I was here first!" she had insisted.

"Go away! Grow up!" Lukas had told her over and over when he wasn't teasing her because he knew her face would get red and she would fight back.

But it was worse when she did grow up. She got curves—and breasts. She traded in her pigtails for a short shaggy haircut that accentuated her cheekbones rather than her freckles. She made her already huge blue eyes look even bigger with some well-placed eye shadow. She got her braces off, wore lipstick and sometimes actually smiled.

But never at him.

Except…sometimes, obliquely, Lukas thought she watched him the way he watched her.

But her focus was always on Matt. "I'm marrying Matt." Holly had said that for years.

Hearing her, Lukas had scoffed. And at first Matt had rolled his eyes, too. But he had never been mortified by her declaration as Lukas would have been.

"That's Holly," he'd said and shrugged. Then, when he was fourteen, he told Lukas that he'd kissed her.

"Holly?" Lukas felt as if he'd been punched. "You kissed Holly?" Then, hopefully, he'd asked, "Was it gross?"

Matt's face had turned bright red. "Nope."

It couldn't be different than kissing any other girl, Lukas had thought. So he'd done that. And then he'd kissed another. And another. He couldn't believe Matt kept on kissing only Holly.

Then, Christmas of Holly's senior year in high school, they'd got engaged.

"Engaged?" Lukas hadn't believed his ears. It was ludicrous, he'd told Matt fervently. He'd told Holly the same thing. "You're crazy," he'd said. "How can you think about spending the rest of your life with one person? You're not in love!"

But they hadn't paid any attention to him. And when he'd tried to make it clear to Holly, well, let's just say she hadn't got the message. In fact, she'd hated him even more.

Then, when Matt was twenty-two and Holly just twenty, they had tied the knot.

Lukas had been on the other side of the world when he got Matt's call to come home and be his best man.

"I'm in Thailand!" Lukas had objected. He'd been crewing on a schooner that summer, basking in sunny days, balmy nights and the charm of a bevy of intriguing, exotic women. He hadn't been home for three years, had no intention of going to the wedding.

"There are planes," Matt had said. "Get on one."

Lukas had argued, but Matt was implacable. "You're my best friend," he'd insisted. "You've always been there, always had my back."

The words had stabbed his conscience. "Fine," he'd muttered. "I'll come."

He'd done it. Had even managed a toast to the happy couple at the reception. Then he'd got the hell out of there, lying about the departure time of the plane he had to catch. He'd been back in Thailand twenty-four hours later—back to his real life, back to being footloose and fancy-free. Matt could have marriage with its boredom and sameness.

Lukas had been telling himself that for a decade now. Today was no different, he thought as he shaded his eyes with his hand and squinted out across the water. It was just a matter of putting the past to rest.

And then he saw her.

One minute he was scanning the water where everyone pretty much looked alike paddling their canoes and kayaks and pedal boats in the confines of the marina. The next moment his gaze locked onto a woman in the back of a canoe out near the breakwater. There were two kids in front. And in the back there was Holly.

His heart kicked over in his chest. He didn't know how he'd missed her before. There was, as always, a purposefulness about her. Everyone else was splashing and floundering. Holly was cutting through the water with ease and determination, as if she knew what she wanted and aimed to get it.

She hadn't changed a bit.

He remembered when she hadn't known how to paddle a canoe, and, taking advantage of that, Lukas had refused to let her come with him and Matt.

Her chin had jutted. Her eyes had flashed. "I'll learn."

He'd scoffed. "From who?"

It turned out his oldest brother, Elias, was no proof against big blue eyes. Elias had taught her, and the next time they went canoeing, Holly had come, too.

Suddenly there came a whistle from the car park. A man wearing a green St. Brendan's T-shirt waved broadly. "Bring 'em in!"

With greater or lesser skill, the paddlers turned their canoes and kayaks and headed for shore. Lukas kept his eyes on Holly. He could see her talking to the students,

giving instructions to back off a bit and let the earlier ar-
rivals dock first.

She still hadn't seen him, but she was close enough now
that Lukas could study her more easily. Gone were the luxuriant dark waves she'd worn at her wedding. Now she had
the same pixie-ish look she'd had as a child. Most of her
face was hidden behind a pair of sunglasses and she wore
a sun visor for shade, as well. The boy in the front of her
canoe said something that made her laugh. And Lukas's
breath caught in his throat at the husky yet feminine sound.

"Gimme a hand, mister?"

Lukas looked down to see a kayak alongside the dock
and two boys looking up at him. One held out a line to
wrap around the cleat. Lukas crouched down to steady the
kayak while the boys scrambled out. Then he helped them
haul it out so they could carry it up to the waiting van. Out
of the corner of his eye, he kept an eye on Holly's canoe
where she was talking to her students. She was still several feet away from the dock.

One by one, as the canoes and kayaks came up against
the dock, Lukas helped them all until finally when he
turned back there was just one canoe left.

Holly sat in the stern, unmoving, her sunglass-hidden
gaze locked on him. No question that she'd seen him now.

Lukas straightened nonchalantly. "Holly," he said casually. "Imagine meeting you here."

The boy and girl in the canoe looked at him, surprised.
Holly's sunglasses hid her reaction. She still didn't move
as the two students brought the canoe against the tires
lining the dock, and Lukas grabbed the bow to hold it
for them.

The boy scrambled out, followed by the girl. Holly
stayed where she was.

"Thanks, mister," the boy said.

"You're welcome." Lukas had seen all the St. Brendan's canoes now, and this one, with its deep, narrow hull, was far nicer and swifter than the wide-bottomed trio he'd helped pull out earlier. He let his gaze slide slowly over it, then brought it to rest on the woman who hadn't moved. "Nice canoe. Yours, Holly?"

"How come you know Ms. Halloran?" the girl demanded.

"We grew up together—I've known Ms. Halloran since she was about your age."

The boy's brow furrowed, as if he couldn't imagine either of them being that young. "You kiddin'?"

"Not kidding." Lukas held up three fingers. "Scout's honor."

"You were never a Boy Scout!" Holly blurted.

"Ah, she speaks," Lukas drawled.

Her freckled cheeks were suddenly a deep red.

"I was a Cub Scout," Lukas said, "when I was eight. You didn't know me when I was eight."

Holly gave a muffled grunt. She still didn't move to get out.

And knowing her, she probably wouldn't, unless Lukas forced the issue. "Nice to see you again, too, Hol'. It's been a long time." He held out a hand to help her out of the canoe, daring her to refuse it.

She muttered something under her breath that sounded like "Not long enough."

And of course, she ignored his hand. Instead, she set the paddle on the dock and shoved herself up, trying to step sideways at the same time so as to avoid his outstretched hand.

In a flatter-bottomed canoe, it might have worked. In this one, she'd barely edged sideways when the canoe tipped.

"Oh!" she yelped. "Oh, hel—"

"Ms. Halloran!" The kids shrieked as Holly pitched, arms flailing into the water.

Lukas couldn't hide the unholy grin that stretched across his face.

More kids came running. So did the men loading the canoes onto the trailer with St. Brendan's van. Lukas didn't move.

Holly sputtered to the surface, hair streaming, sunglasses gone, those all-too-memorable blue eyes shooting sparks in his direction. He still couldn't stop grinning.

All around him kids clamored. "Ms. Halloran! Are you okay?"

"Ms. Halloran! You fell in!"

"You're s'posed to stay in the center of the canoe, Ms. Halloran!"

One of the men who'd come from the van pushed past Lukas, a hand outstretched to help her. "Are you all right?"

"She's fine," Lukas said abruptly, stepping around the man and reaching to grasp her arm. He hauled her unceremoniously up onto the dock, steadying her with a hand against her back, aware of the warmth and suppleness of her body through her wet T-shirt even as she shivered. "Aren't you fine?" She sure as hell looked fine, her nipples pebbling beneath the cotton of the shirt and her bra. He swallowed.

"Of course I'm fine," she said brusquely, clearly unaware of the spectacle she presented as she turned to the students. "I slipped. We've all done it, haven't we?"

At the fervent bobbing of heads, Holly grinned, shaking her hair out of her eyes. "So, I'm just today's reminder. Do what I say, not what I just did. Now, let's get the canoe out." And with a deft move, she twisted out of Lukas's grasp to haul the canoe up onto the dock.

If the T-shirt was a temptation, it was nothing compared to the way her shorts plastered to her rear end. Lukas's mouth went dry. The other men and boys seemed to be appreciating the view, as well.

Stepping between Holly and her interested audience, Lukas wrested the canoe away from her, simultaneously snapping at one of the teachers. "Get her a towel. The rest of you, give me a hand."

Everyone jumped to obey, and by the time Lukas and the boys wrestled the canoe onto the dock, Holly was wrapped in a towel.

The man who had provided it held out a hand to Lukas. "I'm Tom. Thanks for helping her out."

Lukas grinned. "It has always been my pleasure to pull Holly out of the water."

"Usually after you pushed me in," Holly retorted.

Tom blinked. "You two know each other?"

"We're old friends," Lukas said.

"He's an old friend of my husband's," Holly amended. "Lukas Antonides."

Tom Williams beamed. "Great. He can take you home then."

"I ride the bus!" Holly protested.

Tom raised doubtful brows at her sodden clothes and streaming hair. "They aren't going to let you on like that."

"I'll take a taxi."

Tom shook his head. "Not likely, Hol'."

"It's all right," Lukas said. "I'll take her."

Tom beamed and grabbed Lukas's hand, pumping it up and down again. "I wouldn't want to leave her to get home on her own, and I've got to get these kids back to school. See you Monday, Hol'. Come on, gang." He clapped two of the boys on the shoulder, then herded all the kids up to the van.

Holly didn't speak until they were all out of earshot. Then she said, "I'm not going with you."

"Right," Lukas said. "You're just going to stand here until you dry."

He could hear her grinding her teeth. She didn't look at him, just hugged her towel tighter and stared at the departing van. Lukas didn't care. He stood there and drank in his fill of Holly Halloran.

It felt oddly like reaching an oasis after a lifetime of wandering in the desert. He had spent so many years determinedly not thinking about Holly that it was hard to believe she was actually here in front of him.

She was definitely no less eye-catching than she had ever been. Her bones were sharper now, her eyes set deeper. Tiny lines fanned out at the corners of them. From laughter? From sorrow? God knew she'd suffered that. Lukas wanted to reach out a finger and touch them.

No doubt he'd get a slap for his trouble. That wouldn't have changed, either. Except once. Once she'd let him touch her.

"What are you doing here, Lukas?" Her voice cut across his memories, jerking him back to the present. She was looking at the Manhattan skyline, not at him. There was nothing inviting in her tone.

"You wrote me a letter," Lukas reminded her.

Her fingers tightened on the towel wrapped across her breasts. "I sent you a deed of gift and asked you to sign it. Or to tell me if you wanted to keep the boat yourself."

"I read that."

"So, I repeat, what are you doing here?" The afternoon sun made her hair look more auburn than brown, like spun copper.

"I figured we could talk about it." He paused. "I wanted to see you."

Wanted to see if whatever he'd once felt was still there. It was perverse, he supposed, how Holly's contrariness had always sharpened his senses. Going head-to-head with Holly always exhilarated him, made him feel alive. As a boy he hadn't understood the subtext to their encounters, hadn't yet connected the dots. It was all about attraction. His brain had finally recognized it at fifteen. His body had known it sooner—probably from the very moment he'd met her when he'd been shaken and stirred, both at once. He'd put it down to the suddenness of her tumbling out of the tree and confronting him. His heart had pounded and his pulse had raced the same way they were doing now.

The way they had the night he had incurred Holly's everlasting wrath, the night he'd crossed the line.

And heaven help him, Lukas wanted to cross it again. He'd been gone for a dozen years, had dated more women than he could even remember, and they'd all paled in comparison to Holly. His best friend's girl, and he'd never stopped comparing other women to her! He wanted to touch her again now, wanted to feel the softness of her skin and to trace her curves, to kiss her lips and still the chatter of her teeth. Good lord, her lips were blue!

"Come on," he said abruptly. "Let's get you home."

"I don't need you to—"

"Don't be an idiot, Holly. I'm offering you a ride. Nothing else!"

For the moment.

For a dozen years he'd told himself that the past was past, that they'd all moved on, that what he'd felt was kid stuff, that he was well over her. After all, when he'd come back to New York, he hadn't sought her out. He hadn't even considered opening that door again. Not until Wednesday when he got Holly's letter.

And when the door had opened anyway, he knew he

had to see her again. But even this morning he had been convinced that everything he'd ever felt for Holly wouldn't stand the test of time. She had been the dream girl of his past, the one girl against whom he'd measured all the others he'd met since.

But he really hadn't expected to do more than make his peace with the past—with her. He expected to feel maybe a little nostalgia—and a twist of guilt.

But seeing her now, he knew it wasn't going to be as simple as that. He felt the guilt, all right. But he didn't feel nostalgia.

He felt as fierce an attraction as he'd ever felt. Some elemental connection that he'd never felt to another woman. He had a lot more experience now than he'd had back then.

Yes, she was obviously still holding a grudge. But he had to believe she'd changed, too, that she couldn't hate him forever. Could she?

Lukas slanted a glance at the girl who had stirred his blood, at the woman apparently capable of stirring it still, and knew he was going to stick around and find out.

For all that he suspected he should, he couldn't walk away.

CHAPTER THREE

THE MINUTE SHE saw Lukas, Holly had felt her heart kick over in her chest. All the years of pretending he didn't exist blew right out the window. It was like being eighteen again—young and intense and, above all, foolish.

And there was nowhere to run. Nowhere at all.

For years every time Holly remembered the night of her senior prom, she had done so with a bucket load of guilt—and a heart load of resentment.

It never should have happened, she told herself. And it was all her fault.

She should have been stronger. Firmer. She should have said no, right from the start, when Matt had broken his leg.

At least it hadn't been her fault he'd broken his leg. That had, of course, been Lukas's—just as every hair-raising, death-defyingly stupid thing Matt and Lukas had ever done could be laid squarely at Lukas's door. In this case, two weeks before her prom, Lukas had persuaded Matt to climb Mount Katahdin in Maine.

Holly had not been invited.

She couldn't have gone anyway because, while Matt and Lukas were sophomores in college and their sched-ules that Friday were free, Holly was a senior in high school with classes every day. Besides, it was the week-end she was getting her dress fitted for the prom, not to mention that her mother would have freaked out if Holly ever dreamed of going camping with two guys, even if one was her fiancé.

Lukas thought their engagement was idiotic. He had looked confused, then appalled when she had held out her hand to show off her ring. "What's that?" he'd asked warily.

And when she'd said, "I'm engaged," he'd stared at her in disbelief.

"To get *married*?"

"No, to wash windows." Holly had rolled her eyes. "Of course to get married. What do you think?"

He had thought they were out of their minds, and he hadn't hesitated to say so. He'd told Matt he was foreclosing on his options too early, that he had no idea what other women were on the planet, that he would never know what he was missing. He didn't tell Holly anything. Obviously he considered Matt to be the one making the bad choice. She'd wanted to smack him.

But Matt—her dear, dependable Matt—had just laughed and said, "I'm not missing anyone important. I've got the only one who matters." And he'd wrapped an arm around Holly's shoulders, hauling her hard against him, the two of them presenting a solid wall of defiance in the face of Lukas's scorn.

Only then had Lukas turned to Holly. "You can't be serious." His tone had said he wasn't joking. Their gazes met and something flickered between them that Holly immediately suppressed. Attraction? Connection? She had never let herself examine it too closely. Lukas Antonides was far too powerful, too unpredictable—too intensely *male*—for Holly to handle.

"I love Matt," she had said flatly. It was true. Matt was comfortable, predictable—every bit as male as Lukas, but without the intensity she found so unnerving.

Lukas hadn't disputed it. But he hadn't shut up, either. Over the following weeks he had told her she was too young. He'd questioned whether she knew her own mind.

Deliberately Holly had turned a deaf ear. "What do you care?" she'd asked.

If he'd said, "I love you," what would she have done? Holly laughed at herself for just thinking it. Lukas love her? Ha! Lukas had been going through girls for years!

He'd scowled then. "I don't want you making a mistake."

"I'm not making a mistake."

But Lukas didn't seem to agree. As winter turned to spring, he'd found ways to keep them apart. In February he and Matt had bought the battered old sailboat in New Haven. It wasn't seaworthy. It would have sunk in a bathtub, but Lukas had convinced Matt they could repair it.

"It will take months," Holly had pointed out. And that would be if they worked on it every weekend, which would mean Matt would have less time for her.

"We can sail around the world after we graduate," Lukas had gone on, undaunted.

"I'm getting married when I graduate," Matt had reminded him.

Lukas had shrugged dismissively. "Who knows what will happen in a couple of years. You can at least help me work on it," he'd said to Matt.

So, good friend that he was, every weekend that spring, Matt had worked with Lukas on the boat. Holly had barely seen him. The one weekend he had said he would come home turned out to be the weekend she was doing the final fittings on her prom dress.

"No problem," Matt had said. "Lukas wants to go to Katahdin."

Feeling hard done by, Holly had said shortly, "Let him."

"He wants me to go, too. It'll be a change from working on the boat. And you're going to be busy anyway."

So Matt had gone—and had broken his leg. Which was how Holly had ended up with Lukas as her date to her senior prom.

"I won't go," she'd told Matt. "No way."

Matt had looked at her from his hospital bed, foggy-eyed with anesthetic. "Of course you have to go. You already have your dress," he reminded her the day after he'd had half a dozen screws and a plate put in his left leg. "You've been counting on it."

"I don't mind staying home. Truly. Lukas doesn't want to go with me. He doesn't even like me."

"Of course he likes you. He's just…"

"Bossy? Opinionated? Wrong?"

And though she could still see the strain and pain on Matt's face, he had laughed. "All of the above. It's just the way he is. Ignore it. It's your prom. And Lukas should take you," he added grimly. "It was his idea to go climbing. He owes me."

No doubt about that. But Holly was sure Lukas would refuse. She was stunned when he didn't.

"Why?" she'd demanded suspiciously.

"Because he understands responsibility," Matt said, looking completely serious.

She should have said no then. She hadn't, telling herself that arguing with Matt would make him unhappy. It might also make him wonder why she was protesting so much. Holly wouldn't even let herself think about why she was protesting so much.

She didn't want to think about Lukas, about how when he wasn't irritating her, the very sight of his muscular chest, lopsided grin and sun-tipped shaggy hair made her blood run hot in her veins.

It meant nothing. She was engaged to Matt.

Still, she wasn't prepared two weeks later when she opened the door to Lukas, drop-dead gorgeous in a dark suit, pristine white shirt and deep red tie, for the impact of six feet of walking testosterone. The sheer animal magnetism of the man made all Holly's female hormones flutter in appreciation while her brain screamed, *No! No, no, no!*

But she could hardly send him home. What would she tell Matt?

So she pasted her best proper smile on her face and tried to pretend she was completely indifferent. Yes, he was gorgeous. Yes, he smiled and chatted and charmed her mother. Yes, he brought her a corsage, which he fastened just above her left breast, standing far too close for comfort, so close that she could smell a hint of pine in his aftershave and see the tiny cut on his jaw where he'd nicked himself shaving.

She leaned toward it instinctively, then jerked back, practically getting herself stabbed by a florist's pin in the process. "Sorry," she muttered, mortified. "Sorry."

He just smiled his engaging Lukas smile, the I'm-so-sexy one she had seen him turn on other girls but which until that moment he had, thank God, never turned on her.

"It looks good on you," he said. It was a spray of tiny deep red roses. Delicate and aromatic. She drew a breath, trying to draw in the scent of roses to blot out the pine of his aftershave, to blot out Lukas.

But Lukas wouldn't be blotted.

Worse, he unnerved her by being a perfect gentleman the whole time. He didn't tease, he didn't mock. He didn't mention Matt or their engagement at all. He took her to dinner before the dance. It was expected. And Holly had thought they would go to one of the trendy upscale local places where most of her classmates went to see and be seen. But Lukas took her to a quiet romantic Italian place where he seemed to know everyone.

Holly couldn't help looking surprised.

"We don't have to go here," Lukas said. "But I like it. It's a little lower-key."

Since when was Lukas lower-key? But Holly had nodded, glad they weren't in the midst of a crowd. There might have been safety in numbers, but there would also have been lots of questions about what she was doing with Lukas, why she wasn't with Matt.

They'd get asked at the dance, of course, but they wouldn't become a conversation piece there. Holly didn't want to be a conversation piece. "It's fine," she said. "I like it." She managed her first real smile of the evening then, one that didn't feel as if it had been welded to her lips.

Lukas smiled, too. Electricity arced between them— sharp and frighteningly genuine. "I'm glad," Lukas said.

Holly wasn't sure if she was glad or not. Tonight Lukas was everything Matt had assured her he would be: polite, charming, an easy conversationalist. When the waitress brought their menus, he didn't tell her what she ought to order. He asked what she'd like to eat.

It was a sort of dream date—an intoxicating, heady experience. Unreal, almost. Holly kept waiting for him to revert to the Lukas she was accustomed to, but he never did.

At the dance, when she expected he would do his duty, dance once or twice with her, then disappear with the more interesting, flashier girls, he stayed by her side all evening. She wondered aloud whether he wouldn't rather dance with other girls, but Lukas simply shook his head.

"I'm happy," he said as the music started again. Without another word, he swept her into a dance while Holly's mind spun and her body responded instinctively to Lukas's powerful lead. One of her hands was gripped in his hard, warm fingers, more callused than Matt's, rougher to the touch, giving her another tiny stab of awareness. Her other hand, resting on his shoulder beneath the smooth, dark wool of his suit coat, felt the shift and flex of strong muscles.

When she danced with Lukas, her eyes were on a level with his lips. Instinctively she licked hers and stumbled, red-faced, at where her thoughts were going.

"What's wrong?" Lukas pulled her up and held her closer.

"N-nothing." She tried to put space between them, averted her gaze from his lips. "What're you doing?" she demanded as Lukas only drew her closer.

"It's called leading." The soft, almost teasing murmur in her ear sent a shiver to the base of her spine.

He led. She followed. Their bodies touched. The experience was nothing like the warm, slightly zingy buzz she experienced when she and Matt danced. No, each touch with Lukas felt electric, a shock to the system, a different sort of awareness altogether.

"Relax." He breathed the word in her ear on a warm breath that did anything but relax her. She felt alert, aware, awake as she'd never been awake before. Expectant—though what she was expecting, she would not have dared to think.

Lukas didn't say anything else, just moved with the music, drawing her with him, easing her closer. His hand slid to her hip, but went no farther. And gradually, unable to remain alert and wary every moment, Holly realized that she was relaxing. She found joy in the movement, in the rhythm, in the warm nearness of Lukas's body. He made her feel oddly protected.

They danced almost every dance, far more than she ever would have with Matt, who much preferred to stand on the sidelines and watch while he talked sports with the guys. But Lukas danced. And eventually he began to talk, too, recounting what they had been accomplishing on the boat, then telling her what they had seen mountain climbing in Maine.

"So you don't think breaking his leg is all we did." His smile was wry.

Holly gave him a doubtful look, but she couldn't help smiling and sharing a moment of rapport with Lukas. He asked her about her classes, and he surprised her by talking about his own courses.

"I don't know what I want," he said. "I just try things. See what I like. I've got geology this semester that is kind of cool. And—don't laugh—but I like Latin. But what the hell do you do with Latin?" He shrugged. "What about you? What are you going to do?"

Holly, disarmed by Lukas liking Latin, found herself telling him about her own plans and dreams. "Nothing grandiose. I want to get married, have a family. I've always wanted kids."

"Me, too," Lukas said. Another surprise. "Not anytime soon, though," he added quickly. "Not ready to settle down yet."

She wasn't at all surprised by that. "Before I have kids, though," she went on, "I think I'll teach."

"You'll be good at it," Lukas said. And when she raised a questioning brow, he shrugged. "You should be able to handle a classroom. You always kept me in my place." His wicked grin flashed, inviting her smile in return, and Holly did.

The whole evening was like that—Lukas attentive and fun to be with—a Lukas that once upon a time she had dared to imagine might lurk beneath his teasing, baiting, infuriating exterior. But if that Lukas ever even existed, he'd seemed far out of reach.

She shouldn't even be thinking about him that way. She was engaged! She was going to marry Matt!

So she deliberately closed her eyes and tried to pretend that he was Matt. But the aftershave was wrong, the way he moved on the dance floor was smoother, easier. His height was wrong, too. She opened her eyes again at the feel of something feathery touching her forehead and saw Lukas's lips so close they could kiss her brow. Holly sucked in a careful breath and shoved the thought away.

Why were there so many slow dances tonight?

Holly longed for something fast and furious to burn off her awareness, to give her some space. But when the next one was fast, it was no better. Seeing Lukas's body shimmy and thrust to the music while she did the same, created something elemental, primeval, between them.

Holly tried to deny it. It was only dancing, she told herself. But their bodies were in sync, moving, shifting apart, coming together. And at the end Lukas grabbed her hand, then spun her out and reeled her back into his chest so that his body spooned against hers as he wrapped her in his arms.

"Oh!" Holly's body was trembling, her heart hammering. His hands cradled her breasts. One of his legs had slid between her own. Holly tried to get her balance, to pull away. But her overheated body wanted nothing to do with that. She turned to stare breathlessly up at him.

Lukas was breathing hard, too. His cheeks were flushed, his forehead damp, his hair tousled across his forehead. Her fingers itched to brush it back, to feel its silkiness between her fingers. Deliberately, she knotted those fingers into fists.

"Hot work," he muttered. "Let's get something to drink."

"Yes." Before she went up in flames.

He got them each a soft drink, and they stood watching as the next dance began. It was a slow one again. Romantic. If they danced now, Lukas would pull her into his arms. Holly felt her body trembling.

"Let's sit this one out." Lukas's voice was gruff.

"Yes." Holly nodded and took a desperate gulp of soda, praying that it would cool her down. But nothing cooled her down that night. Amid the kaleidoscope of lights and sounds, of fast dances and slow, she was seduced by the moment, by the night. She told herself it wasn't Lukas making her feel this way. But she had to admit he had made it a night to remember. He'd been the Lukas she'd dared to dream he could be.

When the prom ended, several friends were heading off together for a late meal. Had she been with Matt, no doubt they would have joined them. Holly expected Lukas to breathe a sigh of relief, bundle her into his car and take her straight home.

But when her friend Lucy called over, "Do you guys want to come to Woody's?" Lukas had looked at her.

"Do you?"

She hadn't expected that, and was ready to say no, sure he'd had enough of the evening, of her. But before she could answer at all, he went on. "That's what you do on prom, isn't it? Stay out till dawn?"

Stay out till dawn? With Lukas Antonides? An inappropriate flutter of anticipation tickled her. "Well, I—"

He raised a brow. "Would you go with Matt?"

"Sure, but—"

"We'll come," he said to Lucy. He slanted Holly a grin. "After all, I'm standing in for Matt."

So they went to Woody's, an upscale version of a fifties diner, full of her classmates, all laughing and talking, still on a high from the dance. Lukas, to her surprise, fit right in. He talked sports and surfing and sailboats with the guys. He was easy and charming to their dates.

They squashed into a booth with three other couples. Holly would have been comfortable with Matt shoved in next to her, would have relaxed when he slipped an arm around her. But when Lukas did it, she could feel every inch of the hard muscles of his arm. She was more aware of the heat of his body pressed hard against her than of anything anyone was saying.

She was sure Lukas wasn't aware of her with the same intensity. His knee bumped hers, then finally settled against it, and he didn't seem to notice. He kept right on talking to Sam, Lucy's date, even as his fingers played with a strand of her hair. If she turned her head even slightly, her lips would brush his fingers. Holly shivered and looked straight ahead. It didn't mean a thing. It was just Lukas. He didn't mean anything by it.

But her whole body was thrumming with awareness by the time they left Woody's. The noise subsided when the door shut behind them. The night breeze on her heated skin made Holly shiver.

"You're cold," Lukas said. "Here, have my jacket." He made to shrug out of his coat.

Wear Lukas's suit coat still warm from his body? Holly shook her head quickly. "N-no, thanks. I'm fine. It's lovely out here, isn't it?" She did a pirouette in the parking lot, looking up at the night sky, trying desperately to get her bearings, to get her feet on the ground.

Lukas glanced up briefly, then looked straight back at her. "Not as lovely as you."

Holly stared at him in shock. Was she losing her hearing? Imagining things? "Was that a compliment?" she ventured.

"I can give them," he said gruffly.

"Not to me."

His mouth twisted. "Don't let it go to your head." Now he sounded more like the Lukas she'd always known, but perhaps just a little bit kinder. Then, like the gentleman he had never been until that night, Lukas opened the car door for her, then shut it once she got in.

"You know, one of the things I hated most about you—" she said when Lukas got in and shut the car door.

He had been about to put the key in the ignition. Instead, he stopped and looked at her, startled. Then a corner of his mouth quirked up. "Just one? I'm sure you have a whole long list."

She did, but this was one she felt compelled to share. "Yes, but listening to you guys talking back there reminded me of this one."

Lukas raised a brow, waiting for her to speak.

"I hated that you wouldn't let me go sailing with you. You used to take Matt out with your dad and your brothers, but you wouldn't take me." She probably shouldn't even be admitting that it had mattered.

Lukas looked thoughtful, then he nodded, put the key in the ignition and turned it. The car hummed to life, but he didn't put it in gear immediately. Instead, he stared straight ahead in the dimly lit parking lot as if making up his mind about something. Deciding if he should apologize? That would definitely be un-Lukas-like.

Finally, he turned to her. "You want to go sailing? I could take you sailing."

"When you and Matt get your boat finished?" Holly said with a tiny smile. "The twelfth of never?"

"No. Now." There was a rough edge to his voice. And though it was dark in the car, Holly could feel his gaze on her as if he were touching her.

"Now?" she said doubtfully. "Tonight?"

"Don't want to take the boat out in the dark. But when it starts to get light... How about that? We'll end the night with a sail." And he gave her one of those amazing Lukas Antonides grins that would have caused a saint to cave in to temptation.

Holly was no saint. Besides, it was just sailing, she told her sensible self, the one that was telling her to say no. He was, for once, being kind. It was Lukas's way of making up for years of thwarting her. Was she supposed to throw it back in his face?

Besides, she did want to go sailing.

And with Lukas? Well, this had been Matt's idea. Not hers.

He was playing with fire. Lukas knew it.

But he'd never been one to play it safe. And he hadn't started this. It had been Matt insisting that he take Holly to the prom. What should he have done? Said no?

So he'd done it. He'd done everything Matt would have done—taken her to dinner, danced every dance with her, put his arm around her in a crowded restaurant to make more room for her friends. And if he had heightened his own desire with every touch, well, he could see desire in Holly, too.

He had seen the way she'd looked at him tonight. Her cheeks had been flushed, her nipples had become hard pebbles beneath the midnight silk she wore. Lukas was twenty years old, not a virgin. He knew something about the response of women's bodies when they were aroused. Holly had been aroused. By him. And God knew he was aroused by her.

He should take her home. She was Matt's girl. Not his. He had no right. But what if she was making a mistake

marrying Matt? What if she wasn't as in love with Matt—
as committed—as she believed she was?

Don't go there, Lukas told himself.

But he couldn't bring himself to take her home. He'd offered her a sail. It wasn't betraying Matt to take her for a sail.
Lukas put the car in gear and headed toward the marina.

Halfway down the dark, narrow highway, Holly said,
"I can't."

Lukas, shoulders tense, turned his head sharply. "Can't
what?"

"Go sailing! How can I in this dress?"

He breathed a sigh of relief. "No problem. There's stuff
on board. Shorts, T-shirts. Jackets. You can wear something of Martha's. It'll be fine."

She swallowed. "Oh. Well, good." She didn't sound
wholly convinced.

Lukas expected she would find another reason to call
a halt to things. But as he kept driving, Holly was silent.
She sat very still the rest of the way.

The marina parking lot was virtually deserted, allowing him to park next to the ramp leading to the dock.
Some cars were still there because people had taken their
boats out for the weekend. But no one was around. Lukas
started to lead the way down the ramp, then realized that
Holly had to pick her way carefully because she was wearing high heels.

He went back and swept her up into his arms.

"Lukas!" She wriggled against him.

His half arousal went to full-on just like that. His jaw
tightened. "You want me to drop you? Stop squirming!"

"I can walk," Holly protested.

No. He wasn't relinquishing her now. He strode down
the ramp, getting a faceful of hair and a breath of citrus
shampoo for his effort. "Hold still!"

"I am!"

She was. He was the one who was moving, causing her body to rub against his. Lukas swallowed a groan. By the time they got to the boat and he let her slide down his body to put her feet on the deck, he was in a state of temptation and torture both. It was worse to let her go.

"Martha's stuff is below," he said gruffly, leading the way down to the galley where he pointed to one of the tiny bunk rooms. "Put on a bathing suit. We can go for a swim."

Holly looked at him, startled. "Swim?"

"There's a beach just on the other side of the shop." Lukas jerked his head in that direction. "We've got a couple of hours to kill before it starts to get light." He could think of other more pleasurable ways of killing that time, but he knew better. He needed cold water. Lots of it. Now.

He thought she would object, but after a second's hesitation, Holly nodded. "Good idea."

When she disappeared into one room, he went into the other and stripped off his clothes, grateful for the cool night air on overheated skin. Then he dragged on a pair of board shorts and went back up on deck where he stood staring up at the sky, his body rock hard from a combination of desire and tension, as he wondered again what the hell he was doing with his best friend's girl.

"Just doing what he asked me to do," Lukas muttered aloud. Matt would have kept her out all night, he reminded himself. It was what you did after prom. It was a tradition. Matt wouldn't have taken her for a sail, though. Matt had nothing to take her for a sail in.

No, Matt and Holly would have been doing something else entirely. Lukas cracked his knuckles fiercely, trying to avoid thinking about Matt and Holly making love when he so badly wanted to do it himself.

It was almost a relief when Holly climbed back up the steps. Except the sight of her—even in Martha's sensible one-piece maillot—was enough to cause his self-control to slip another notch. Even the fact that she had a towel draped over her shoulders with the ends hanging down in front shielding her breasts from view didn't help. Her long legs were bare and tempting in the moonlight.

Lukas sucked in a breath and jumped back onto the dock without waiting for her. "Come on," he said over his shoulder and headed back toward the parking lot and the beach on the other side of the closed shop as fast as he could.

The whole place was deserted. But the moon and the lights in the parking lot illuminated the steps so that finding their way down to the beach was easy enough. He walked ahead, needing the space, only stopping to wait for her at the edge of the water.

She didn't come. Instead, when he looked back, Holly had spread her towel and was sitting down.

"Sunbathing?" Lukas, self-control fraying badly, couldn't keep the edge from his voice.

"Guess so." Holly pulled her knees up toward her breasts and wrapped her arms around her shins. "Don't let me stop you. Go on in."

Lukas stared at her. What the hell was she playing at? Maybe she knew he was coming undone and was giving him a wide berth. "Suit yourself," he growled. Then he turned and ran, flinging himself under the incoming wave.

The shock of the cold Atlantic in the middle of an early May night had the desired effect. By the time he broke the surface, he breathed a little easier. A glance back told him that Holly had stood up and was walking to the water's edge. He caught a glimpse of a long, lissome shape in the moonlight. Then she began to run into the water.

He heard a shriek, then she dove under—and surfaced bare inches from him.

So much for dampened ardor. Lukas swallowed a groan.

"It's freezing!" Her teeth were chattering.

He resisted wrapping his arms around her. "You'll warm up. Come on. Let's swim." He took off, swimming away from her as he'd always done, never letting her catch him. And Holly swam after him.

Minutes passed. Half an hour. They did laps. They swam in lazy circles. Lukas finally slowed a bit to allow her to come alongside where she did the sidestroke, all the while keeping her eyes on him.

Lukas couldn't take his eyes off her. He should say something about Matt. Something to deflect his awareness, but nothing deflected his awareness of the girl swimming mere feet away. It reminded his fevered brain of one of those nature films they had showed in school, the ones that euphemistically described the mating rituals of exotic maritime animals. Not a useful train of thought. But apparently the only train of thought he had. It was all he could do not to reach for her.

"You're making me crazy," he muttered at last and abruptly turned to swim back toward the beach.

"What?" Holly sputtered. "What's wrong?" He could hear her splashing after him, but he didn't wait. Lukas needed space. He needed distance. He needed to stop wanting what he couldn't have. He didn't stop moving until he was back on the boat.

Then he turned to see Holly hurrying up the beach and across the parking lot after him, her towel wrapped around her shoulders. Her teeth were chattering like castanets when she finally reached the boat.

"Why didn't you say you were cold?" Lukas demanded. "You can take a shower." He slipped down the steps below deck and jerked open the door to the head. "There's plenty of hot water. Lots of towels. Get warm, I'll be on deck."

He changed swiftly into another pair of shorts and a sweatshirt, resolutely ignoring the sound of the shower and his imagination's notion of Holly's naked body beneath the spray. Instead, he made himself focus on getting the boat ready to go. He was checking the mainsail when he heard Holly's footsteps.

"What did you mean?" she said. Her voice was quiet.

He turned around then. She was wearing shorts and a baggy sweatshirt of Martha's that hit her midhip. They had never struck him as remotely sexy when Martha wore them. Put Holly in them and it was a different story. Lukas crouched down, showing sudden interest in the mast again, in case his interest in Holly was more obvious.

"You said I made you crazy." She had climbed up on one of the benches and was almost on eye level with him.

Lukas shrugged awkwardly. Was he supposed to tell her he wanted her? That he was crazy with longing for her—and she was engaged to his best friend? He put a hand back and rubbed between his shoulder blades and said the only thing he could think of. "You always argue."

"I didn't argue tonight!"

He grunted. "Most times you argue."

"So do you."

Lukas scowled, unable to dispute that. He turned his attention back to the mast. "We can go soon. Should begin to get light in half an hour or so."

He thought she might go away, look out to the east for signs of dawn. She didn't. She watched him. Then she asked, "Why did you agree to take me to the prom?"

"You know why. Matt asked me to." He flicked a quick glance up at her, then picked at a bit of loose brightwork with his thumb.

"Is that the only reason?"

His brows drew down, and he scowled at her. "Why else would I do it?"

Holly shrugged awkwardly. "I don't know. I just…wondered. Sometimes…" She stopped and looked away, staring out across the dark water. "Never mind."

Wondered what? Don't stop there! But damn it, she did. She didn't say anything else. And he couldn't make himself ask. He and Holly never had heart-to-hearts. They never talked about things that mattered. And he wasn't going to admit to anything when she wasn't saying how she felt.

"That's the only reason," he said gruffly. "I'm just doing what Matt would do. What Matt wanted me to do."

If he said it out loud firmly and flatly enough, would that make it true?

"Of course." Holly's voice was toneless. Was she convinced? Was she doubtful?

Did she want…him? Lukas rubbed his hand against the back of his neck, then he straightened, walked back to the cockpit and dropped lightly into it. Only one way to find out. He reached up and caught her hand, pulling her down off the bench to stand facing him.

"What?" Holly looked up at him, confused.

"What would you and Matt be doing now?"

Her eyes widened. "What do you mean?" She looked at him, confused and wary.

"You asked me a question. My turn to ask you one. I'm standing in for Matt, aren't I? What would you and Matt be doing?"

He felt her fingers twist in his as she looked away. "How should I know?"

"Kissing?"

She didn't answer, just pressed her lips together and refused to look at him.

"Kissing," Lukas affirmed softly, leaning in, so close now that he caught another hint of that citrus scent.

Her fingers pulled out of his hands. He let go, but only to catch hold of her wrists, then slid both his hands up until they rested lightly just above her elbows, drawing her closer.

"So I haven't been doing my job," he said, keeping his voice even, although he felt the tension rising within.

He would burn in hell for this. He knew it, but he couldn't help it. If she responded... If she wanted him, he would save her from making the biggest mistake of her life.

Holly flicked a quick glance up at him, then immediately looked away again, but it was too late. Lukas had seen a flicker of interest in that glance. He let go of her arms to touch her face, to turn it to look at him as he ran his thumbs along her jaw and slowly and deliberately lowered his mouth to hers.

Lukas's brain fogged over. His body took over. He had no plan. Hell, he never had a plan. He went with his gut— and other even more interested portions of his anatomy— doing what came naturally, tracing her lips lightly with his tongue. Teasing, testing, tasting...

And Holly didn't pull away.

The taste of Holly on his lips intoxicated him, made him tremble with the need that had been building all evening. Evening, hell, it had been building for years. From a time when he was too young to understand, some gut-level instinct deep inside him that he couldn't begin to put a name to had zeroed in on her. He had wanted Holly before he'd barely known what such desire meant.

And it hadn't gone away—ever. No matter how hard he'd tried to make it, no matter that she belonged to Matt, no matter how many other girls he'd dated, kissed, touched in an effort to blot Holly out of his mind, she was still there. He couldn't explain it. Couldn't begin to try. He only knew it felt right to have Holly's mouth open under his, to have her body pressed against his, driving his need higher.

He would stop. Of course he would stop. But not now. Not yet. He had been denied so long. But just now, just for the moment, he needed this. Needed her. If she wanted to stop it, she would.

But Holly didn't pull away.

Instead, as his thumbs caressed her temples and his fingers tangled in her hair, Lukas felt her lips part more, allowing him to deepen the kiss, to slide his tongue between her lips, to touch hers.

If she'd pressed her lips together, he would have stopped. If she hadn't opened to him, if he hadn't caught the sound of a sigh escaping her and felt her tremble at his touch, he would have stepped back, let her go. But instead, she lifted her hands and laid them against his chest.

And she didn't push him away. On the contrary, her fingers curled into the fabric of his sweatshirt, clutching him close, hanging on.

Lukas moved closer, trapping her hands between them as his lips traveled along the line of her jaw, nipping, tasting. His fingers stroked down over her back, then slid up beneath the baggy borrowed sweatshirt to settle against silky-smooth skin.

There was the slightest hitch in her breath, but when he began an easy, gentle stroking, she arched into him, her spine elongating, as if she welcomed his touch.

Lukas welcomed being able to touch her. No doubt about that. He'd wanted to touch her forever. But the closest he'd come had been when he'd pulled her pigtails or pushed her underwater. Except once. When she was fourteen they had been biking and she'd hit a rock, falling, hurting her wrist and gashing her leg. It was obvious that she couldn't ride home. So, leaving Matt to bring her bike, Lukas had carried her.

Holly hadn't argued about it. She'd let him take charge, hadn't resisted when he'd pulled off his T-shirt and wrapped it around her leg, then lifted her into his arms.

It was the only time he'd held her until tonight.

This was far better. Now he could run his hands over her back, relishing the lack of a bra that would have impeded his fingers' journey. He could slide his palms around to cup her breasts and nuzzle them beneath the soft cotton of the sweatshirt. Now he could trace the line of her spine and the waistband of her shorts. So he did.

And Holly didn't push him away. Instead, she drew her hands out from between them, but only to set them on his hips. She leaned closer and tentatively brushed her lips along his jawline. Everywhere her lips touched Lukas felt little sparks of electricity.

He groaned as hot blood pounded in his veins and he felt the thrum of wanting build within. But more than he wanted to take Holly, he wanted to know her, wanted to feel her tremble beneath his hands, and know that she was responding to him.

He sank onto the bench where she'd stood earlier, then drew her down onto his lap, into his arms, and kissed her again, even more deeply this time, tasting her, savoring her as she squirmed against him, curving her body into his.

Her bottom shifted against his erection, making him even harder than he already was. His hands were unsteady as they stroked their way up her legs. She moved again, settling in, and Lukas had to edge his legs apart to ease the pressure just enough to keep from disgracing himself completely. Then he slid a hand around and up across her rib cage to find the soft swell of her breast again.

He cupped it in his palm and felt the nipple pebble as he rubbed his thumb over it. Holly whimpered and shifted under his touch, rubbing against him through the thin cotton of his shorts. Lukas's eyes squeezed shut.

But his hands kept moving, kept exploring. He drew lines up her thighs to the hem of her shorts, across the tops, down the sides. He drew circles on the insides of her knees, then his fingers ventured slowly up her inner thighs. He felt her breath quicken. His fingers slid back down and circled around her knees. His heart pounded in his ears.

He could hear hers, too, as his explorations grew bolder. His fingers skated under the hem of her shorts. Then they slid back down. He heard her swallow. She shifted, but she didn't protest. She seemed to be alert, attentive, waiting. Wanting?

Wanting what he wanted? Lukas eased her around so that she curved toward him, one of her feet on the bench, her knee bent, the foot dangling off where she sat on his lap. Now when his fingers slid up her legs, he had room to explore, to learn the warmth and softness of her inner thighs, to venture farther to the lacy edge of her underwear.

Holly didn't stir. Only her breathing quickened as Lukas explored the lacy boundary, stroked along it, then dipped beneath.

Holly sucked in a breath. He felt her tremble. Or was that him?

Lukas had had sex before, but not like this. He'd been in too much of a hurry before, too eager for his own pleasure, unaware—for his sins—of the girl he was sharing it with.

He wasn't unaware of Holly. Yes, his body was clamoring for completion, but Lukas ignored it, more interested in Holly than in himself. What would make her tremble? What would make her moan?

He desperately wanted to know Holly's mysteries, wanted to bring her pleasure even as he made her his own. So his fingers trembled as he parted her and touched the warm wetness of her. He knew what that wetness meant. It made him harder than ever. His fingers slipped between her folds, stroked her, and reveled in the way she arched against his touch, making a sound deep in her throat.

He wanted to tear her clothes off, and his. He wanted to plunge into her and take her with an urgency he'd never before been able to control. But tonight he forced himself to go slow, to give, not just to take. To draw a response from Holly even as his whole body trembled with the need of her. Then he heard it again—another whimper, and she was no longer holding perfectly still. Her hips had begun to rock in counterpoint to the rhythm of his stroking. Her thighs parted, giving him greater access.

Eagerly, Lukas took it, reveled in it. It didn't matter now what his body wanted. He wanted this—for her.

It was only moments until Lukas felt Holly begin to tremble against the stroke of his fingers. She shuddered, her hips rocking, her breaths coming in quick gasps. Then her whole body seemed to ripple as tremors coursed through her, rapidly first, then gradually abating as she buried her face against his shoulder.

Lukas cupped her, didn't let go as he felt tiny after-shocks against his fingers. In his lap Holly barely seemed to be breathing now. He could feel her heart hammering, but she didn't move. On the knife's edge of desire, Lukas didn't move, either. Didn't even breathe. Just waited.

Dared to hope.

Then, as if she were just discovering that she could move her limbs, Holly began to move. Her movements were stiff, almost if she were coming back to life. Then her fingers uncurled from his sweatshirt and abruptly she shoved herself away from him, wobbling as she stood.

Lukas reached out to help her get her balance, but she jerked away, wrapping her arms across her breasts. "Take me home." There was a hoarse, almost desperate edge to her voice. She didn't look at him.

"What?" Lukas stared at her, stunned. "Take you—? But—"

He reached for her again, but Holly twisted away.

"I want to go home." Holly's voice was low and shaking. She tried to move past him toward the stern. "Now."

Lukas blocked her way and caught her by the arms. This wasn't the way it was supposed to happen! "Why? What's the matter with you?"

Holly lifted her face and gaped at him. "What's the matter with me? You don't know? You have no idea? You just— We just—" Her voice was shrill. He'd never heard it like that before.

She didn't finish the sentence, just yanked her arm out of his grasp and pushed past him, scrambling over the side of the boat and onto the dock. She set off toward the car, barefoot, never glancing back.

Lukas stared after her, dazed, confused, and still aroused enough that it almost hurt. He couldn't even move, and she was practically running. She stopped at the car, opened the door, jumped in and banged it shut after her. If she'd had the keys, no doubt she'd have driven off and left him there!

What the hell was wrong with her? He hadn't done anything she hadn't wanted! She'd had every opportunity to say no. It wasn't as if he'd actually *done* anything—as his body was only too willing to complain about!

Lukas winced and swore under his breath as he began to move about the boat, gathering up her dress and shoes, and his own clothes. His arousal began to abate a bit, but his fury and bafflement were growing exponentially as he stuffed his feet into a pair of deck shoes, then began to close up the boat. He took his time, grinding his teeth the whole while.

Only when he was sure his dad wouldn't even know he'd been here did he head back to the car. Holly was sitting in the front seat, looking mutinous, staring straight ahead. It was hard to equate her rigid, icy posture with the girl who had minutes before melted in his arms.

It wasn't hard. It was impossible.

Lukas tossed her dress and shoes on her lap. "You forgot something." His voice was bitter, ragged, raw. He couldn't help it.

Holly wadded them into a ball and wrapped her arms around them, still refusing to look at him.

Lukas flung himself into the driver's seat and stuck the key into the ignition, but he didn't turn it on. He just sat and stared at her for a long moment, willing her to face him, to talk to him, to admit that she'd wanted him just as much as he wanted her.

But Holly clearly wasn't admitting anything. Jaw tight, arms hugging her dress and shoes, she just said again, "Take me home."

He didn't move. "You're going to pretend it didn't happen?" he demanded. "It happened."

"I didn't *want* it to happen!" In the harsh glare from the lights of the parking lot, her eyes spat fire. "I love Matt!"

Lukas felt her words like a blow to the gut.

"You did, though." Holly's eyes glistened. Were those tears that were accusing him? "You got what you wanted, though," she said bitterly. "Didn't you?"

And wasn't that the joke of the century?

What *he* wanted? He wanted Holly understanding—and

welcoming—his feelings. He wanted Holly recognizing her own feelings for him.

Had he got that? Not even close, Lukas thought, his throat tightening. Yes, those were tears brimming. As he watched, one slid down her cheek.

Perilously close to crying himself, Lukas didn't bother to answer. He started the car.

In silence, he drove her home.

CHAPTER FOUR

LUKAS LEFT THE next morning.

Thank God his father, intending to go to Greece on family business, had jumped at the chance to send Lukas instead.

So Lukas had never had to face Matt, had never been forced to lie to his best friend's face about what had happened that night. He'd lain awake for hours after he'd dropped Holly off. He'd spent them tossing and turning, reliving every moment, aching with unfulfilled desire as well as the growing guilt and shame that came with finally admitting to himself that he'd misjudged everything, that he'd betrayed his best friend.

It was a blessed relief to get to the airport, to put miles between himself and the scene of the previous night's debacle and the people he didn't want to face.

He didn't call Matt. Instead, he sent a text from the airport, explaining the trip to Greece was a business emergency, that there was no choice, he had to go.

It was the truth.

But the bigger truth was that he didn't want to face Matt. And he couldn't face Holly.

He was raw and aching, and he could barely think about what had happened the night before without flinching away from the memory. He'd been so gratified at her response, had barely believed it was happening, yet at the same time thought he was proving a point. If she was responding, she had to realize that she couldn't blithely marry one man when she had feelings for someone else. For him.

But evidently she hadn't. She'd been furious.

So why had she let him touch her if she felt that way?

Lukas never did figure that out. And he sure as hell had no one to ask. Finally, he told himself it was just one of the mysteries of women. But it hadn't helped.

God knew what Holly thought of him after that night. Lukas didn't want to know. He knew what he thought of himself—that he had betrayed them all that night by taking what he wanted, by being selfish and immature and greedy. He couldn't have Holly. He had no right to her.

She didn't love him. She loved Matt.

Lukas felt sick.

The family business on Santorini had taken all of five days, but afterward Lukas hadn't gone back to New York. He'd stayed the whole summer in Greece building boats with his grandfather and crewing for a company that rented high-end sailboats for vacationers on the Mediterranean.

And while he stayed away, a tiny part of him dared hope that Holly would realize in retrospect what she hadn't realized that night—that she loved him.

But by autumn he knew it wasn't going to happen. He never heard a word from Holly. And all he had from Matt was a handful of emails. The first had thanked him for being a good sport and taking Holly to the prom, the second said that Holly reported that they'd had a good time, the third wondered when Lukas was coming home so they could work on the sailboat.

So Holly had never told Matt what had happened.

Lukas supposed he should be grateful that Matt didn't want to punch his lights out. Instead, he just felt guiltier. His other feelings—the ones towards Holly—hadn't changed. He tried to think about other women, deliberately—and desperately—losing himself in the lure of every passably attractive woman who smiled at him.

At the end of summer, he didn't go home at all.

Sometimes Lukas told himself he was being noble, refusing to go back and make Holly uncomfortable. In truth, he knew he was making himself as comfortable as possible by staying away. He couldn't face them. He had ostracized himself.

He hadn't gone back at all until Matt demanded he be best man at their wedding.

It was his punishment, Lukas realized—to attend their wedding, to stand there and watch Matt and Holly stare into each other's eyes as if they were the only two people in the world, then to have to reach into his pocket and hand over the wedding ring that Matt slipped onto Holly's finger. He'd even had to prepare a speech that he'd rehearsed so often he could say it in his sleep.

Matt had been amazed. "You? Prepared?" He'd laughed at the thought.

But sheer preparation was the only thing that had got Lukas through it. Then he'd toasted their happiness. He didn't dance with the bride.

"Sorry," he said right after the toast as he headed toward the door. "I've got a plane to catch."

He caught that plane and then another. He drank more whiskey than he should have, hoping it would take the edge off his pain. It hadn't. But he'd survived. He put all thoughts of Holly behind him. That chapter of his life was over.

He hadn't let himself look back.

When he heard of Matt's death, he had felt guilty and gutted—and he'd stayed away. He'd never let himself think about Holly unattached.

Until now.

And now, Lukas thought grimly, it was déjà vu all over again. The old turmoil was back. The awareness. The desire.

He had spent the past half dozen or so years growing up, becoming the adult he probably should have been then. He had focus these days. Purpose. He worked hard. He made better than a good living. He gave back to the community. He dated sophisticated, sensible women. Beautiful women like Grace Marchand.

And he was still hung up on Holly.

And Holly still hated his guts.

He looked at her now as she stood on the dock, arms folded, holding the towel across her chest, shivering with cold, determinedly ignoring him.

He didn't blame her.

"Come on, Holly," he said to her now. "Your lips are turning blue. Let me give you a ride home." He paused. "And an apology, as well."

An apology?

From Lukas? That would be a first. And for what?

As far as Holly was concerned Lukas Antonides had about a million things to be sorry for. She hesitated, wanted to hear more. But, typically, Lukas wasn't waiting around to explain. He was already striding ahead of her toward the parking lot, obviously expecting her to follow.

Holly darted her tongue out at him, feeling childish. Then, as he knew she would, she followed.

Walking behind Lukas was never a hardship. A woman would have to be dead not to appreciate the physical Lukas

Antonides. In casual khaki cargo shorts and a faded red T-shirt, he should have looked no more imposing than the teachers she'd kayaked with from St. Brendan's. They worked out at the gym, but they seemed like milquetoast compared to the man moving ahead of her.

Lukas was lean with broad shoulders, narrow hips and hard muscular arms and legs that spoke of hard physical labor, not a gym membership. He moved up the hill with the grace and power of a panther at home in—and in charge of—his world.

But then, Lukas had always been in charge.

And he had always been gorgeous, with defined cheekbones, a strong jaw and deep-set gray-green eyes. But the angles and planes of his face were harder and sharper now.

The only thing soft about Lukas was his hair. It was still a memorable mixture of dark brown tipped with light, sun-streaked blond, though the blond wasn't as evident these days since his hair was trimmed neatly, shorter than the shaggy mop she remembered. He was still tanned, though she suspected that owed less to days on the beach or on boats and more to the natural olive tones of his complexion.

He had reached the parking lot now and turned for the first time to glance back and make sure she was there. The sun caught the dark stubble on his jaw, giving it a hint of the same burnished gold highlights in his hair.

Trust Lukas to turn stubble into an art form.

Matt would have laughed if she'd told him that. Then he'd have admitted wryly that Lukas probably could.

"He's the best-looking guy I know. Hands down," Matt had always said. "All the girls want him."

"Not all," Holly had been quick to reply.

"Not you," Matt had said wonderingly. He had always shaken his head at that, as if her choice amazed him.

But she had, deep down inside. She'd been as susceptible as all the other girls, even knowing Lukas as well as she did. The difference was she knew herself, as well. She knew, as a girl, that she could never handle a boy like Lukas. And so, while she had the occasional dream of domesticating the panther, she knew better than to try.

That was why his teasing got under her skin. It was like he knew she hankered after him and wanted to bait her at every turn. It was easier—not to mention smarter—to focus on the boy she trusted: Matt.

She should have remembered that the night Matt had deputized Lukas to take her to the prom in his place. If she had, she wouldn't have succumbed to Lukas's charm. She wouldn't have relaxed in his presence. She wouldn't have let him do what he had done.

Even now, a dozen years later, what Lukas had done that night—what she had *allowed* him to do—still mortified her. Her face still burned at the memory.

With a cooler head, she understood why he'd done it. He had railed at them about the stupidity of their engagement since Christmas. They were too young, they didn't know their own minds, they might marry the wrong person, they might not be the right person for the other...

And that night he'd set about proving it—to prove to Matt that he never should have asked her to marry him, that she must not really love Matt because, if she did, how could she have been tempted by another man?

She had let Lukas touch her. In the heat of the moment, she had foolishly allowed him to run his hands over body, to evoke sensations that she'd never felt before. Color her stupid, all right, Holly thought, but those sensations had caught her unaware.

It wasn't as if she hadn't made love with Matt. Before Christmas when they had talked about marriage, about commitment, about being together forever, they had made love.

The first time had been intense, but hurried, and—for Holly at least—unfulfilling.

Matt, while he had known more about lovemaking than she had, hadn't really understood the intricacies of how a woman's body responded to arousal. His own had responded fast and furiously, while Holly had been left feeling vaguely dissatisfied, as if there were something missing, something she hadn't experienced yet.

Something more.

Holly had never quite found that something more—until the night she'd gone to the sailboat with Lukas.

That night things had been different.

Lukas was different.

And when he'd kissed her, she hadn't said no. She hadn't pulled back. She'd been curious. Would it be different from kissing Matt? She had so little experience with other men, she wanted to know.

If Lukas had come on strong, she'd have had the good sense to pull away. But he had moved slowly, taken his time, actually made her eager with anticipation.

Get on with it, she'd thought. That was what a fool she'd been!

Until that night she hadn't understood that slower was better, that every deliberate touch just heightened her awareness, her expectation.

With Lukas expectation became all. The feel of his lips on hers had made her heart beat faster, the stroke of his tongue on hers sent shivers of longing through her.

And his hands—dear God—his hands on her body had made her quiver in response, the slow journey of his fingers over her breasts, then up and down her legs setting off waves of responsive desire that she had only barely begun to experience with Matt.

And that had been her undoing.

With Matt, there had been no opportunity for leisurely exploration, no chance to really learn what pleasures their bodies could give them on the way to climax.

Until the night Lukas had taught her.

Lukas! *Not* the man she loved. *Not* the man she was engaged to.

No, it had been his best friend—and, after that night, *her* worst enemy!—who had brought her to orgasm and had held her in his arms while she trembled and shuddered—then came to her senses and realized what they had done.

Humiliated and furious, feeling she'd been taken advantage of at the same time she knew she had allowed it to happen, Holly had been terrified that Lukas would go straight to Matt the next morning and tell him what she'd done.

She'd been shocked to learn later that day that he had actually left the country only hours later. He hadn't gone to see Matt at all.

Why hadn't he? Had he expected her to 'fess up and break off the engagement herself, knowing that she'd betrayed Matt? If she didn't, would Lukas tell him what had happened?

For days, weeks, months after that awful night, Holly had expected the other shoe to drop. Feelings of panic fluttered in her stomach every time Lukas's name came up. But he never came back.

And as far as she knew he had never said a word.

She was aware that she was holding her breath as she watched him walk down the row of cars. Consciously, carefully, she let it out. She had to stop overreacting to him.

She wasn't a kid anymore. And whatever he did now, he couldn't hurt her anymore. He couldn't tell Matt what had happened between them.

She hadn't wanted to see him again. But now that he was here, maybe it was a good thing. One more bit of the past she could put to bed before she moved out to her coral atoll and discovered the path for the rest of her life.

She took a deep breath, then let her gaze follow him, looking for the Porsche mentioned in the *What's New!* article. His "dream car," he'd called it. A vintage model, green and low-slung and more powerful than a pride of jungle cats. The sort of car alpha men drove.

But even as she scanned the row, Lukas stopped next to an old stake-body truck, its back end half loaded with drywall and lumber.

"Come on," he called to her as he opened the passenger door to the truck.

Holly stopped, then blinked. "That?"

"I didn't bring the Maserati," he drawled. "You'd get the seats wet."

She gaped as she walked toward him. "You have a Maserati, too?"

"No. I have a Porsche. But I drive the truck, too. Easier to haul stuff when I'm working."

Holly's brows lifted.

"I'm restoring a building."

"Yes. I heard. Althea told me about it. And…I read the article," she admitted. "It's how I knew where to write to you." Holly felt self-conscious saying it, but refused to allow it to show. "You've done very well," she added, and then her cheeks did burn because she sounded so…judgmental. And prim.

Lukas's mouth quirked in a sort of wry self-deprecation. "Who'd a thunk it?"

"I didn't mean that!"

"No. I don't suppose you did. Surprised my mother, though. She always thought I'd come to a bad end."

"She did not!" Lukas's mother doted on all her children. Still, when Holly reflected on Lukas's childhood, she realized that between the broken windows and the broken bones, Mrs. Antonides probably had had moments of despair.

"Let's just say she's happy that her worst fears weren't realized." Lukas was clearing off the passenger seat as he spoke, removing a couple of paint cans and some tools. He stowed them in the back, then pulled out a towel, handing it to her. "In case you want to dry your hair."

Holly took it doubtfully. "You carry towels?"

"For a lot of years I never knew when I was going to see running water and indoor plumbing again, so I learned to take advantage of every opportunity."

"Of course you did," Holly replied drily, then realized he could read something else into that comment.

And had, for he cleared his throat. "Like I said, I owe you an apology for that."

Holly lowered the towel so she could peer at him over the top of it.

Lukas looked as uncomfortable as she'd ever seen him. There was a hint of red across his cheekbones. "I shouldn't have…taken advantage." There was serious color in his face, which amazed her. Was he embarrassed?

He hadn't seemed embarrassed then. He'd acted like he was mad because she'd been upset.

"It was my fault, too."

He shoved his hands into the pockets of his shorts. "It didn't feel like it was somebody's *fault* at the time."

"I shouldn't have let it go there." She pressed her lips

ANNE McALLISTER 75

together firmly. "You never told Matt," she ventured after a moment.

"Of course not." He looked indignant now.

"I did," she said after a moment.

Lukas's face went even redder. "You told him?" He looked aghast.

"Not...not everything," Holly muttered, her own face hot now. "I thought you still might, and I didn't want him to learn it from you."

Lukas was still sputtering. "You told him we..." But he didn't finish.

"I said...you'd kissed me." That was enough. She raised her chin defiantly and glared at him.

Lukas dragged in a breath, then pulled his hands out of his pockets and dragged one down his face. He swallowed. "That's all you told him?" He sounded somewhere between wary and relieved.

"I didn't give him a play-by-play," Holly said, annoyed. "I didn't think he'd want to hear it."

"No," Lukas replied with feeling.

"But I didn't want it hanging over me, either, in case you decided to come back and rat on me."

"I would never have—"

"You were friends," she said quietly. "He didn't deserve that."

Lukas was wearing sunglasses so she couldn't read his gaze, but she saw his Adam's apple move, and he dipped his head, acknowledging her words. His jaw tightened. "No, he didn't. I had no right."

"No, you didn't." Holly was glad he realized that. "But it happened. So—" Holly shrugged as indifferently as she could "—I thought, 'I'll just tell him about the kiss. We'll laugh about it.' So I did."

Lukas's hand wrapped around the top of the truck's

door frame, his knuckles white. "And did you?" he asked roughly. "Laugh?"

"We did." She didn't tell him how hard it had been to make a joke of it. But Matt would never have believed his best friend would have crossed the line. And he had given her way too much benefit of the doubt, as well. One of the things she loved most about Matt—and one of his biggest failings—was his tendency to believe the best of people always.

Lukas didn't speak for a long moment. His expression was unfathomable. Finally, he drew a breath. "Well," he said lightly. "No harm done then."

"No."

Not unless you counted Holly's mortification at knowing she had shared with Lukas something she hadn't yet shared with Matt. Later, thank God, she and Matt had learned to please each other.

But Holly could never forget that Lukas had been her first.

CHAPTER FIVE

She was living in the same high-rise condo in Brooklyn that she and Matt had been in last time Lukas had been back in the country. He had been there briefly when he'd picked Matt up to go out for a beer.

Holly hadn't been there, of course. But Matt had shown him around the flat. It was small but modern, stylish and with spectacular views across the East River toward Manhattan. Lukas had wondered at their choice because he'd always imagined them returning to Long Island and raising a family. Maybe they would have if Matt had lived. It hadn't been the sort of thing you asked.

Now he wondered what Holly's plans were. In her letter she had said she was "tying up loose ends." Nothing else. And she wasn't saying anything now.

She'd offered directions to her condo, but other than that she hadn't spoken. And once he had tendered his awkward apology—for something he still didn't quite regret—Lukas had gone silent, as well. He didn't know what to say to her. He never had. It was why he'd always taken refuge in teasing, in baiting, because she had always touched something inside him he didn't completely understand.

Worse, she had always seemed to see right through his bravado. He winced inwardly at the thought of her having told Matt even an expurgated version of what had happened that night. And he squirmed more than a little at them laughing about it. But it hadn't destroyed their relationship at least, and with the hindsight of some hard-won maturity, he had to be glad of that. Matt and Holly had been right for each other, as much as he hadn't wanted to see it. They had known better.

He actually found that he was glad he'd been able to apologize, even a dozen years too late.

Lukas could have just dropped her off at the front door. It was clearly what she would have preferred. But he couldn't bring himself to do it. Whatever it was that had attracted him to Holly years ago still persisted. And things were different now. She didn't belong to Matt. So as they approached the condo building, before she could say, *I'll just get out here*, Lukas said, "We need to discuss the deed of gift."

"Why?" Holly looked at him, startled.

"I want to know more about the school, what they're going to do with the boat."

"I'll have Father Morrison send you a brochure on the school, and—"

"I want to talk to you about it."

"When?"

"How about now?"

He thought she'd refuse, would come up with some reason that it wouldn't work. She could have pleaded that she needed to shower and clean up, which she certainly did. But he waited, and finally she said, "I guess you'd better come up then."

She didn't speak the rest of the way up to her flat. Only when they were inside and he was drinking in an atmosphere of cozy simplicity with a world-class view did she say, "I need a shower before we talk. There are books and magazines on the table if you want. I have coffee and tea."

"I'll be all right."

"Well, if you want some, help yourself. The fixings are right there." She nodded toward the countertop in the kitchen on the other side of the bar that separated it from the living room.

But his attention had been caught by a stack of professionally done flyers on the bar. They advertised a condo for sale. Holly's condo.

Lukas picked up one of the flyers. "You're moving?"

On her way toward the bath, Holly glanced back at him. "Yep. In August."

"Find another place?" This one had never seemed like Holly to him. He wasn't surprised.

"No. I'm leaving."

"Leaving?" He frowned. "The city?"

"The country." And Holly gave him the first really bright smile he'd seen from her today. "I'm joining the Peace Corps."

Lukas stared, feeling oddly as if he'd been punched. "You're joking?"

Holly looked indignant. "You don't think I can do it, maybe I'm not tough enough? Not resilient enough?"

"Of course you can do it." Holly was one of the toughest, most resilient people he'd ever known. As a kid she'd taken anything he and Matt had dished out. And as an adult, well, she'd survived losing her husband, hadn't she?

"It's just—" Lukas swallowed—that he'd just got back, that he'd just seen her again. They'd finally made peace. "You live here," he protested. "You've always lived here."

Holly's smile faded. "I don't think 'always' is in my vocabulary anymore."

Oh, hell. Lukas opened his mouth and closed it again. He rubbed a hand over his hair. "So, you're leaving because of Matt? You don't think that's maybe a little drastic?"

"Dying was a little drastic," Holly said wryly.

"Well, yeah, but…" Lukas straightened his shoulders. "He didn't do it on purpose."

"I know that!"

"I know you know. It's just… I'm surprised, that's all. I thought you loved your job."

She gave him a wary look. "How do you know that?"

"Matt always said so. He said you were fantastic at it, that the kids loved you." Every time he'd seen Matt, his old friend had spent much of the time talking about Holly.

Lukas had told himself he didn't want to hear, but he had never changed the subject. In fact, he'd hung on every word.

"I like teaching," Holly allowed. "I like the kids." There was a renewed warmth in her tone, and he remembered seeing that warmth when she'd been with them that afternoon. "They were what kept me sane," she reflected with a wan smile. "After." After Matt's death, she meant. "They needed me. They made me focus on something besides coming home to an empty house. An empty life." She paused again, then her face brightened a bit. "But there will be kids where I'm going. I'm teaching there, too."

Lukas still wasn't convinced. "Where's there?"

"You won't have heard of it."

But when she told him, he had. It was a tiny South Pacific island he hadn't visited, but he knew where it was. Thanks to what happened on Holly's prom night, Lukas had done a lot of crewing in the South Pacific. He knew hundreds of little islands no one in their right mind would go to. He'd been to most of them. "And that's better than St. Brendan's?"

"Not better." She shook her head no.

"Well, then—" Lukas was ready to argue.

But Holly just shrugged. "I can't stay here. I can't do this anymore. It's…what my life would have been with Matt." Lukas could hear the aching loneliness in her voice. He had to make himself stay right where he was, not cross the room to touch her. "I need to find out who I am without him."

The same person you've always been, Lukas wanted to say, but deep down, he understood. Her dreams had died with Matt. She needed to find new ones.

We can find those dreams together. He wanted to say that, too. But he couldn't. He knew better than to push. He had pushed her twelve years ago, trying to make her see what she didn't see at all.

"There's beer in the fridge," Holly told him, "if you'd rather. Excuse me. I need that shower." And she disappeared down the hall, leaving Lukas staring after her.

Holly took her time in the shower, needing to get her mind and her emotions on an even keel. So much for handling the boat issue with her letter to Lukas. Now she had him in her condo instead.

Worse, it wasn't a "boat issue" at all. It was a "Lukas issue"—and it always had been. She couldn't lie to herself any longer.

She had always, deep down, had a thing for Lukas. Not that she'd ever admitted it—not to anyone. Not even to herself. But for the past dozen years she'd been able to pretend it didn't exist because…well, because it hadn't.

She'd loved Matt. She'd married Matt. It had been the right thing for both of them. And if once upon a time she'd entertained brief foolish dreams of a relationship with Lukas, fortunately she'd known better than to believe it could ever happen.

As long as she had known him Lukas had been the most unsettled, least reliable person she'd ever met. If she'd ever been stupid enough to throw herself at him, she knew he might well have taken her up on it. But after he'd had a taste of her, he would have got bored. He never stuck with anything. The article in *What's New!* had made his varied enthusiasms and scattered career sound like positive things—and for an entrepreneur, maybe they were.

But you never built a lasting relationship on that. And Holly knew herself well enough to know that, however much she changed direction now, if she ever started another relationship it would have to be with someone who felt the same deep, intense commitment she did.

"So remember that," she said, gurgling into the spray from the showerhead, "no matter how appealing you still find Lukas Antonides."

Because one glance of him face-to-face told her she was still susceptible.

Fortunately, Lukas wouldn't be around long. They would sign the deed of gift, chat about what he was doing, what she was doing, maybe talk a bit about Matt and the "good old days," and, in a matter of an hour or two, he'd be out of her life.

Tonight she would go out to dinner and a film with Paul and it would all be behind her. It was no big deal.

It was nice—and unexpected—that Lukas had apologized. Apparently, he had done some growing up, too. Good. They could act like adults.

Thinking about it like that—rationally, sensibly—eased the tension in her shoulders, allowed her to take deeper breaths, and by the time she got out, toweled off and dressed again, she was feeling much more in control.

Lukas had made coffee by the time she returned to the living room. She could smell it, and it made her stomach growl. He held a mug in his hands. He nodded at a second full mug on the counter. "Hope you wanted one."

Holly picked it up, glad to have something to hold. She took a sip. "So what is it you want to know?"

He shook his head. "A dozen years' worth of your life? Too much?" He smiled wryly. "Okay, so tell me what this program is all about and why Matt thought it was a great idea to saddle a bunch of kids with a nautical disaster."

"Because a lot of them are disasters themselves," Holly said. She moved to sit in the armchair that Matt used to sit in, wanting his presence to help her articulate what she was going to say. She gestured to the other chair or to the sofa, hoping that Lukas would take the hint. She didn't need him looming over her. Fortunately, he sat down on the sofa and put his mug on the coffee table. But instead of settling back, he leaned forward, forearms on his thighs, fingers loosely clasped, his full attention on her.

"There are a lot of at-risk kids there. Kids who haven't had a lot of chances. They see their little patch of turf and not much else. They don't know what else there is in the world—unless they see it on TV. So five years ago, after we came back from a canoeing trip to the Southwest where we'd seen groups of kids doing what we were doing and having a blast, Matt said, 'The St. Bren's kids would love that.' And it started from there."

"You took kids to Utah?"

"No. We started trying to find places that we could teach them canoeing and kayaking around here." They'd scavenged up used canoes and kayaks as cheaply as they could. "We took a few hand-picked souls to the marina on Saturdays." She shook her head, remembering. "It was a disaster."

Lukas's brows lifted. "Sounds like a good idea."

"Yes, well, they were afraid of the water. Not one of

them could swim. And they didn't want to learn. Too far out of their comfort zone. We were pretty naive."

"You grew up around water. So did I."

"Yes. And we never gave a thought to how far they'd have to go to make that leap. We needed to start on the ground, let them dip a toe in a pool. So we started there. It was a slow process, but eventually we had some kids who could swim. And when they could, others wanted to. And then we started again with the kayaks and canoes. By this time we figured that they benefitted if they were involved with everything, if they were invested in patching canoes and making kayaks water worthy." She smiled. "Matt showed them how to do that. And they got good at it. They like canoeing. They like kayaking. And now they have confidence to try other new things. The boat—well, the boat was just sitting there. He'd given up on you coming back." She slanted a brief glance at him when she said the words. She didn't mean them judgmentally anymore, though she had for years. She had come to accept that Lukas didn't have much follow-through. And, personally, given what had happened on prom night, she was glad he'd stayed gone.

"I couldn't, could I?" Lukas said now. His gaze bored into hers.

Holly met it this time, but she waited for him to explain.

"I'd betrayed Matt. I'd hurt you. I—" he began, but then just closed his mouth and shook his head. "I didn't have much to stay for."

Holly wasn't sure about that, but the way he said it didn't brook any argument. And this was Lukas, she reminded herself. He wasn't known for staying power.

"Well, anyway," she went on, "Matt thought there were some kids who could work together, who could learn some planning and teamwork that way, if they worked on the boat. And he'd work with them. And then he would teach them to sail." She could still remember the light of enthusiasm in his eyes when he'd talked about it.

Lukas still seemed to be listening intently. He didn't interrupt, he didn't jump up to pace around or crack his knuckles or say, *That's a dumb idea.*

All things that the Lukas she remembered would have done.

This Lukas just sat still and waited for her to continue. Holly swallowed and went on. "He had just talked to Father Morrison about it…the week before he died. But he said he had to make sure it was okay with you."

"Of course it would have been okay with me!"

"You know Matt," Holly said. "He did things by the book. You owned half the boat, ergo, he needed to ask you."

But writing to Lukas was something Holly had never felt up to. So she'd dropped the ball.

Now she said, "If it was so obvious that 'of course it would have been okay with you' why are we even having this discussion?"

Lukas shrugged. "I wanted to see you again. I told you that. And yes, you can have the boat. It sounds like a great plan." He settled back against the sofa now and took a long swallow of coffee. "But I'd like to see it first."

Holly stared at him. "See what? The boat?"

He nodded. "It's been a long time."

"Of course." She didn't ask why. Maybe he was feeling a little sentimental about what might have been. "It's at your brother Elias's boatyard. Just ask him."

"With you," Lukas said.

She almost spilled her coffee. "With me? You don't need me there."

"I want you there."

"Why?"

He shrugged. "It feels right."

"And if it feels right, do it?" Holly said acerbically. "Experience has proved that isn't always the best choice."

Was that a hint of color in his face? Green eyes met hers. "Come with me, Holly."

She couldn't tell if it was a command or a request or an invitation. She hesitated.

"Or are you chicken?" And there it was—the calculated, devastating Lukas Antonides grin, the one that had baited her a thousand times. How could she have thought he'd changed?

"You're such a bully!"

There was unholy glee in his eyes. "I'm not forcing you."

"No?" She glowered at him.

Lukas looked absolutely delighted. "Ah, there's the Holly I remember."

The Holly he remembered wanted to kick him. But maybe it was good to keep being reminded that he hadn't changed. He was Lukas, teasing, taunting, playing some game.

Fine. She'd go along with it. She'd get his signature on the line to deed the boat. And life would be back to normal. "Right. Okay. We'll go see the boat." She stood up and carried her mug into the kitchen.

"Now?" Lukas looked momentarily disconcerted.

"No time like the present." If she didn't go now, she'd have to agree to see him again. Lukas had been enough of a disruption for one day. She didn't need another one. She glanced at her watch. It was just past three. And as long as she got back in time for her date with Paul this evening, no problem. She turned and narrowed her gaze at him. "And after you see it, you'll sign the deed of gift?"

"I said I would, didn't I?" He looked offended.

"And of course you always do everything you say you'll do. Like spend a summer repairing a boat?" Holly raised a brow.

Lukas had the grace to grimace. "I'll sign it."

While she put on a pair of sandals, he called his brother to ask about getting into the boatyard, then hung up and said, "We have to run by his place for a key."

Elias lived in Park Slope, not that far from where Holly lived. She said, "I'll wait in the truck," when they drove up in front of his brownstone twenty minutes later.

"Not a chance. I said I wanted the key and Elias said, 'Great. You can stay for dinner.'"

"I can't—"

"Don't worry. We're not staying for dinner." Lukas hopped out of the truck, then came around to open her door. "But this is family. I can't just grab the key and run. It doesn't work like that. I have to go in, smile, ruffle the kids' hair, say how much they've grown." He sounded bored at the thought, but he stood there expecting her to get out of the truck.

Holly hadn't seen Elias in years and she had never met his wife or kids. "How many kids does he have?"

"Four. It's a madhouse." Lukas rolled his eyes. "Prepare yourself."

But there were no little kids at the door, only Elias, who did a double-take when he saw Holly, then grinned broadly. "Hey, Hol'! Long time no see." Ignoring his brother, Elias pulled her into his arms and gave her a warm hug, which she returned. Then he held her out at arm's length and studied her.

"You're coping," he decided, and she remembered that she had in fact seen him at Matt's funeral, but not since.

"I'm coping," Holly agreed.

Elias nodded his approval. "So what're you doing with him?" He jerked his head at Lukas who, apparently used to brotherly disparagement, brushed past them both and went into the living room.

"We came for the key. She's fine. We're in a hurry, Elias."

Elias ignored him. "Everyone's in the kitchen." He looped an arm over Holly's shoulder. "Come on back."

Lukas sighed audibly. "What'd I tell you?" he said over his shoulder as he headed toward the back of the house. "Tallie is not feeding us," he added firmly.

"Whatever you say." Elias just smiled and drew Holly through a comfortable, cluttered living room, past two dogs, a Lego fortress and a bunch of dump trucks, haulers and steam rollers.

Holly gazed around almost hungrily. It was the living room of her dreams—one filled with the joy and photos and chaos of a growing family, like she'd hoped to have with Matt. But before she could do more than swallow the lump in her throat, a trio of boys came swarming down the hall.

"Hey, Uncle Luke! I got a new dump truck. Wanna dig with me?"

"Uncle Luke. We're makin' a robot!"

"Uncle Lukas, wanna see him walk?"

"Unca 'Ukas! 'Ick me up!" This last voice came when they'd reached the kitchen and a little dark-haired girl toddled into the mix and wrapped her arms around Lukas's knees.

Holly imagined he'd be looking for the nearest exit. But his impatience vanished. He scooped up the littlest boy, flipped him up onto his shoulders, then hoisted the little girl up in his arms and gave her a smacking kiss.

"How's my pretty girl?" He nuzzled her cheek and

made her laugh. "Let's see that robot," he said to the older boys, and she could see that his eyes were alight with boyish enthusiasm.

Holly found herself oddly charmed as, still carrying the kids, he crossed the room to where a slender, dark-haired woman with a pixie-ish haircut was taking a sheet of cookies out of the oven. "Hey, Tallie."

Elias's wife was an adult version of the little girl in Lukas's arms. She set down the cookie sheet and threw her arms around him and her daughter. "Lukas! Where've you been? You'll stay for dinner, won't you?"

Lukas gave Holly a "what did I tell you?" look over Tallie's shoulder. "Thanks, no," he said. "We just came to get a key for the boatyard. This is Holly," he introduced her casually. "My sister-in-law, Tallie."

And as Elias's wife looked her over, Holly had the odd feeling that she was being sized up. Her narrow-eyed assessment was nothing like Elias's welcome. It felt almost suspicious, certainly measuring.

Instinctively, Holly straightened and stared straight back at her.

Her action made Tallie laugh suddenly and, still beaming, she swept across the room to envelop Holly in a warm hug. "Glad to meet you at last."

At last?

But before she could ask what that meant, Tallie stepped back and looked her up and down again. "Yes, you look like you can handle him." Then Tallie had turned her gaze on Lukas. "It's about time you brought her around." Her eyes swung back to Holly. "He's never brought anyone around before."

"Not—?" Holly began, confused.

But Tallie smiled at Lukas. "Helena says you're serious

at last. About time. And she is beautiful, that's for sure. But why did I think her name was Grace?"

"I am not serious about Grace! It's my damn family," Lukas said as soon as he had hustled her out of Elias and Tallie's house. "They meddle. They don't know when to shut up." He flicked on the ignition, put the truck in gear and shot away from the curb as if he couldn't leave fast enough.

Holly, who had watched Lukas's face turn bright red when Tallie had mentioned Grace, only said, "Oh." She wasn't surprised that Lukas wasn't serious about Grace, whoever she was. Lukas had never been serious about anyone.

"You hit thirty and they think you ought to be married," Lukas muttered, the color still high along his cheekbones. He flexed his fingers on the steering wheel. Holly saw his jaw bunch and his brows draw down. "My mother likes Grace," he went on. "Thinks she'd make a perfect daughter-in-law."

"Maybe she would."

"Probably she will," Lukas agreed. "But she's not marrying me. I'm not marrying her!"

"No surprise there." Holly's tone was dry.

At her words, Lukas slanted her a glance. "What's that mean?"

"Just what I said." Holly shrugged. "I mean, how many girls did I watch you date? How many more must you have gone through since?"

Lukas grunted. "That was then." He seemed to be grinding his teeth.

Holly didn't see what difference it made. As far as she was concerned, whoever Grace was, she'd caught a lucky break. "Doesn't matter, does it?" she said. "Not to me, anyway."

She expected him to drop it, but he went on. "My mother is starry-eyed. And she likes a good story. The guy I worked with in Australia, the one whose foundation I'm working on here—Grace is his long-lost love's granddaughter. We've gone out a few times and now Ma thinks it would be 'poetic' if I married her. It's not going to happen."

"I believe you."

But he wasn't listening. "Ma wants more grandchildren." His eyes were on the heavy traffic heading out toward Long Island. He sounded aggrieved.

"Of course she does," Holly said equably. "Why shouldn't she?" Her own mother doted on Holly's brother Greg's two kids. She had been sad when Holly and Matt hadn't had kids. Holly had been sad, too. "You seem to like children," she added.

"It's no reason to get married!" Lukas strangled the steering wheel. "And I'm not marrying to please my mother."

Holly thought it unlikely that Lukas would do anything to please anyone but himself. "I'm sure you won't," she said mildly.

Lukas's jaw bunched. He stared straight ahead. "You like kids?"

Where had that come from? Holly nodded. "Yes."

"You don't have any." He sent a quick glance her way. His words were more question than statement. Holly wanted to say it was none of his business. But before she could, Lukas grimaced. "Sorry. None of my affair."

"We wanted kids. Lots of kids. Not at first. After Matt finished his PhD. But we didn't have any. Two years went by and I didn't get pregnant, so we went for tests. Everything seemed okay. The doc said we were 'trying too hard.' He said, 'Relax. You can't plan everything. Some things happen when you least expect them.'"

She glanced at Lukas. He didn't say anything, didn't even glance her way. But she was sure he was listening even though she wondered why she was telling him any of this. It was something she hadn't told anyone at all, not even her mother.

"He was right. Matt died—definitely unexpected." Holly's fingers knotted in her lap. She could hear the blood rushing through her veins, could hear the quickened beat of her heart. "And I miscarried the next week."

His gaze was on her then, searching her expression.

She looked away. "I was a month along. I…I didn't even know I was pregnant until…until I lost the baby."

There was a moment's silence. He didn't say a word. Then he reached over and wrapped his hand around hers.

It was the last thing she expected—warm physical comfort from Lukas Antonides. For once, Holly didn't pull her hand out from his grasp.

"I didn't have any idea," Lukas said at last, his fingers still wrapping hers. "I'm sorry." He hesitated. "No one said. After Matt died, I talked to my mom now and then. She said you were coping. She never said anything about…" His words dried up. His thumb rubbed the back of her hand.

Holly wetted her lips. "She didn't know. No one did."

"No one? Why not?"

"It was…too much." She sighed and tried to explain. "Everyone was already devastated by Matt's death. If I'd said…about the baby… They all knew how much we wanted a family. If they found that I'd lost the baby, too…" She just shook her head. "I couldn't tell them. I couldn't bear any more sympathy."

She knew it sounded strange. Ungrateful.

But Lukas just nodded. "I get it."

She raised her gaze to look at him, surprised. But Lukas's tone was quiet and calm and his fingers continued to squeeze hers in silent commiseration.

Oddly, it felt as if he really did understand. She supposed he might. Lukas had known her—and Matt—for a very long time. And while he might not know them the way their parents had, in some respects he knew them better.

Maybe, too, she had had enough space and time between herself and both excruciating events to actually speak of them and not have the emotions destroy her.

After Matt's death, friends and acquaintances had sympathized fervently, and often awkwardly, unsure what to say to "make things better."

Nothing could. But Holly didn't say that because that would have been rude. Instead, she was the one who ended up comforting them. She couldn't do more of the same after her miscarriage. She didn't have the strength.

Now she didn't need to have strength. Lukas gave it to her. He kept her hand wrapped in his, holding on firmly.

She was holding hands with Lukas Antonides. *Who'd a thunk it?* Holly thought with a wry inward smile. He had rough hands, workman's hands, calloused and competent, quite different from her husband's hands. But even though Holly knew from the article that Lukas's work now was largely behind a desk, he still clearly spent a lot of his time doing physical labor.

"Are you doing all the work on the building yourself?"

He slanted her a quick glance, and seemed to sense that she didn't want to talk any more about Matt or their unborn child. He nodded. Then his gaze grew self-conscious as it dropped to their linked fingers. "You'd think so, wouldn't you?" he said wryly. "But I'm only doing the grunt work. Painting, hauling, whatever the professionals don't do. My cousin Alex is an architect. He did the design for the renovation. And I've got a contractor now. He hires the workers we need. I do the rest."

She imagined Lukas did considerably more than he said. He'd never been a hands-off sort of guy. "What's it like?" she asked.

So Lukas described the gallery space on the first floor, the studios where some of the artists would be "in residence," working while people watched. He told her about the office space and the seven apartments.

"Some are even done," he added with a faint grin. "Mine is. And the one for my gallery manager, Jenn, who's coming on Monday. And two on the third floor. None of them would be finished if I were doing it myself. You should come see it," he suggested.

"Maybe." But Holly knew she wouldn't. Today was a one-off. Get the deed signed. Move on. "I'm getting ready to leave. I have to pack and still make the condo look presentable for potential buyers. I should have started a few weeks ago," she admitted. "But I couldn't get my mind on it until now that school's almost over."

"Haven't they tried to talk you into staying at St. Brendan's?" Lukas asked. "I figured they'd fight like hell to keep a good teacher."

"They asked. But it's time to move on. You should understand."

Lukas raised a brow. "Me?"

"It's what you did," she reminded him. "When you left."

Lukas let go of her fingers and put his hand on the steeling wheel, all the while keeping his eyes on the road. "That was different."

"Different how?"

He didn't answer, just rolled his shoulders in silence. She thought he wasn't going to answer. But finally he said, "It just was."

"So you're not going to talk about it?"

A muscle ticked in his jaw. "I'm not."

"But—"

"You've only got to think about it, Holly," he said gruffly.

She frowned. So, okay, he'd betrayed Matt. He'd said that already. And there wasn't anything to stay around for. He'd said that, too. But he'd left his degree half-done. He hadn't come back. She turned her head so she could look at him, try to see what had been turning the wheels in his head. But as always, what went on inside Lukas Antonides's thick skull was beyond her.

So she turned away and stared out the window. They were nearing the turnoff for the boatyard. The late-afternoon sun had dropped in the sky behind them. It beat on the back of her neck through the truck's window, but it was no longer as hot as it had been earlier. The boatyard was deserted when they arrived.

"I'll open the gate," she said. "The boat is around back of the boathouse. You can park there." She nodded toward a place near the office where she and Matt had parked when they had come here. "I'll show you where it is."

She didn't wait for him, though. It was the memories of Matt, she told herself, that were making her weepy. They had come out here only a couple of weeks before his death. Matt had been so eager to see the boat again, yet had walked slowly, holding back, almost as if he were afraid that it would be beyond repair. She knew he hadn't wanted to get his hopes up. Of course he had talked about Lukas that day, too. *Lukas and I were going to do this*, and *Luke thought we should do that*.

Of course Lukas had never been around to do any of it. But as always, any mention of Lukas had brought back Holly's feelings of guilt.

And now…coming here with Lukas felt like a very bad idea indeed. Behind her she heard Lukas shut the truck's door. Then his footsteps came across the gravel after her.

"Wait up!" he called. "Going to a fire?" he began with a grin when he reached her. But when he saw her face, his grin faded. "What's wrong?"

"Everything's fine. Come on." She started walking again. But Lukas caught her wrist and hauled her to a stop.

"You're crying." He sounded appalled, looking at her worriedly, out of his depth.

"It's okay. I was just…remembering…the day Matt and I came here." She swallowed. "He was so happy. He had so many plans. I…don't usually get weepy anymore. Sorry." She wiped a hand down her face.

"You don't have to apologize." Lukas's voice was gruff. "I didn't mean to bring it all back. Do you want to wait in the truck?"

"No. I said I'm fine."

He didn't look convinced. "It won't take me long. I just…wanted to see it again." He took a breath. His gaze was dark and serious, as if he were intending to lay some ghosts to rest, too. "Come on, then. Let's get it done."

She would have gone along without being held on to. But Lukas didn't let go of her hand, and Holly was exquisitely conscious of the hard strength of his fingers, though he grasped her lightly enough.

Only when they reached the boat itself did he loose her fingers, letting his own drop to his side as he just stared at it. Holly, watching him, couldn't begin to read the shuttered expression on his face.

As she watched, Lukas walked around the sailboat in silence, his expression hooded and unreadable. The boat's name, *Promise*, was still faintly legible on the bow. Matt had traced it with his finger and grinned. "That's perfect for the kids," he'd said. "A promise they can keep."

Unlike the one Lukas had made to you, Holly had thought at the time. She would have bet he didn't even remember it. But now, watching Lukas circling the boat slowly before pausing and hunkering down to examine the work Matt had done on the hull, she thought she'd been wrong. She saw sadness in his gaze. She saw a flicker of pain. Lukas ran his hand over Matt's patching effort.

Holly waited for him to acknowledge it, but he didn't speak. So she did. "Matt did a lot."

Lukas nodded. "Yes. He never said."

"Maybe he didn't want to make you feel like a slacker." It wasn't a kind thing to say. "I'm sorry," Holly said quickly.

"No." Lukas lifted his shoulders. "You're probably right. Will they work on it here at the boatyard?"

"I think so. Elias said they could. Tom, the guy you met, will be in charge."

"When will they start?"

"As soon as we give them the deed. Ready to go?"

"Not quite." Lukas nodded and hoisted himself up into the boat, then disappeared from view.

Holly glanced at her watch and shifted from one foot to the other. It was already after five.

Finally, Lukas reappeared. "Lotta work." He put one hand on the not-very-bright brightwork and jumped lightly back down onto the ground.

Holly nodded. "But it will keep them off street corners and out of trouble." She gave him a bright smile. "So, it's okay? Now you'll sign?" She was pulling the envelope with a copy of the deed of gift out of her tote bag even as she spoke.

A corner of Lukas's mouth lifted. "You're in a big hurry to get rid of me."

"Is there anything else you want to see? If not, I'd like to get back." She held the paper out, then pulled a pen from her bag.

"It's almost time for dinner. I'll sign it at dinner. Where should we go?"

Holly shook her head. "Sorry. I can't."

"Can't?" Lukas's brows drew down. "Or won't?"

"Can't."

Lukas looked skeptical. "You don't eat meals?"

"I'm going out."

"Out?" he said, as if he didn't understand the word. "You're going *out*?"

"I have a date."

A date. Holly had a date.

All day long he'd been treating her with kid gloves, tip-toeing around her very understandable grief for Matt—and all the while she'd been waiting to go out on a date!

Furiously, Lukas slapped paint on one of the gallery walls. Damn her! He tried telling himself that it didn't matter, that he'd lived without Holly Montgomery Halloran for his whole life, that it didn't matter what she did.

But his gut reaction to discovering that she was going out tonight—with a guy who wasn't him—put the lie to that.

"Who is he? What's his name? What does he do?" he'd demanded.

Holly had blinked at his intensity before she'd responded. "His name is Paul. He's a psychologist. A friend of Matt's," she had told him as he'd driven her back to her condo. "He's a good guy. You'd like him."

Lukas doubted that. Now he strangled the brush in his hand, aware he was wishing it was Paul the psychologist's scrawny neck. Rationally, he told himself that Holly was entitled to date anyone she chose.

But it didn't stop the way he felt. Every bit of his possessiveness toward Holly that he had relinquished to Matt's greater claim years ago had come winging right back the moment Holly had said she was going out.

It didn't even matter that she'd told him it wasn't serious.

"We're just friends," she had said almost apologetically as she'd got out of his truck, refusing to let him to do more than pull up at the curb outside her place.

With benefits? Lukas had wanted to demand. But he'd managed to hold his tongue. "Friends?" he'd snarled.

"Yes. We go out together. Do things. Concerts. Ball games. I'm trying to get a life." She gave a vague wave of her hand. Then, at his scowl, she went on, "I'm in a hurry, Lukas. He's going to be here any minute. But—" and here, damned if she hadn't given him a bright cheery smile "—it was great to see you and catch up. Thanks again for signing the boat over to St. Bren's."

Then she'd waggled her fingers and disappeared inside her building as if she fully intended to never see him again!

We'll see about that, he thought as he thwacked the paintbrush hard against the wall.

CHAPTER SIX

"I WON'T HAVE IT!" Holly burst through the door to his office, red-faced and furious.

Lukas swallowed his astonishment—and the leap of his heart—at the sight of her. "You won't have what?" he asked mildly.

It had been a week since he'd seen her. A week in which he'd managed to knock out three walls, paint an apartment, read the best twenty-five grant applications, interview half a dozen gallery assistant applicants, show up at the first session of work on the *Promise* out at the boatyard and dream about Holly every night—sometimes twice.

He had picked up the phone fifty times at least, to call her "just to talk." And every time he'd put it down again because, God knew, he and Holly had never "just talked." But it would have been a place to start.

Now, apparently, he didn't have to. He looked past her toward the open door wondering how she'd got past Sera. Not that he was objecting.

As he did so, Sera appeared in the doorway. "I'm sorry! I was on the phone and she…she just…zipped past."

Lukas shrugged, still enjoying the heightened color in her cheeks. "She does things like that." He gave Sera a commiserating smile. "It's all right. I'll handle her."

"You won't 'handle' me!" Holly slapped her hands on his desk and glared at him. "You *can't* handle me, Lukas Antonides! I'm not Matt. You're not going to ignore me!"

Sera paused in the doorway. "Are you sure, Lukas?"

Lukas, never taking his eyes off Holly, nodded. "It's fine," he told Sera. "I've never ignored you, Holly." *Couldn't. Not even when I wanted to.*

Holly snorted. But at least Sera believed him. With one last worried glance, she backed out of the room. Lukas waited until the door had closed with an audible click, then nodded toward one of two leather armchairs not far from his desk. "Would you like to sit down? Can I get you a cup of coffee?"

"No, I wouldn't like to sit down! And I don't want coffee. I'm not staying. This is not a social call!"

"I gathered that," he said drily. "So what's the problem?"

She hugged her arms across her breasts. "I won't let you do to the kids what you did to Matt!"

Lukas sobered instantly. "What are you talking about?"

"You went to the boatyard yesterday."

"So?" That was a bad thing? He'd rung up Father Morrison on Monday and asked when they were meeting. He'd been intrigued by the idea of working with them—and tempted by the thought that Holly might be there. She hadn't been. But he'd still found the kids' eagerness compelling, and they'd been thrilled to learn about his connection to the boat.

"Why?" she demanded.

"Why not?"

"Because you're raising expectations!" Holly's voice began to rise again, too. "They'll expect you to come every week!"

Lukas tilted his head. "So?"

"So it won't work. You'll go a few times. Make them count on you—and then you'll drop them."

"No. I—"

"It's what you do, Lukas," she insisted, cutting him off. "It's what you always did. You always started something, then didn't finish it."

"The hell I—"

"You did," she insisted. "Remember the go-kart you and Matt were going to build?"

She'd had to go back a long way for that one, Lukas thought. He'd been eleven.

"And what about when you were going to learn to scuba dive?"

"I did learn," Lukas protested. "Just not then." The three of them had signed up for scuba lessons one summer in high school. But then his dad had asked him to go to Santorini to help out his grandfather for the summer. How could he turn down his grandfather?

"And then there was the sailboat. One minute you were full of plans, fixing it up, sailing around the world, and the next you're off to Greece for something better to do!"

"We both know why I had something better to do, Holly."

She stepped back as if he'd slapped her. She took a breath and let it out slowly before saying in a voice that wasn't quite steady, "So this is...*my* fault?"

Lukas shoved himself up out of the chair. "Of course it's not your fault! It's *my* fault! I told you that! But you know *why* I went." One of the reasons, at least.

She hesitated, then gave him a tight little nod. "So, am I supposed to thank you for leaving?"

"You could," Lukas said drily, "but I don't expect it."

Holly grunted and paced around his office. If she were a cat, Lukas thought, she'd be twitching her tail in fury.

It reminded him of all the times she'd railed at him when they were kids. He'd been fascinated by her. She was so intense. So loyal. No one had more spirit than Holly. No one championed the underdog the way she did.

She had reached the end of the room and turned back to face him again. He could see her working to get herself under control. "Look," she said at last, "it's simple. I told you lots of these kids have had a rough time. They've been let down more than once. They need to be able to count on people."

"Got that," Lukas said.

"Which means if you act like you're going to be there, you have to be there."

"I'll be there."

"You might intend to be there—you might have intended to stick around and work on the boat, I don't know—but things happen!" Her face suddenly grew bright red again. No doubt they were both remembering exactly what "thing" had happened that night. "You run a damn empire now, Lukas! How do you know you won't have to dash across the world to do something important?"

"Because I run a damn empire, and I decide what's important." He met her gaze implacably with one as fierce as her own. "And if I say I'm going to be there, I will."

Their eyes dueled. Holly didn't give an inch, but Lukas wasn't backing down. It was obviously more important than he realized that he follow through with the kids. And admittedly, he hadn't given it a lot of thought when he went in the first place. Now he could see her point. He wasn't totally self-absorbed. He had grown up.

Still she stared into his eyes. He stared right back. Finally, Holly broke eye contact. She pressed her lips together and looked away across the rooftops of SoHo.

Outside, Lukas heard a siren. In Sera's office the phone

rang. She'd better deal with it herself. He wasn't picking it up if she put it through.

"I'm not going anywhere," Lukas repeated. "I get it, Holly. I understand. And I *can* make time. I *will* make time." He raked fingers through his hair, then dropped his hands to his sides. He paused, once more letting his gaze lock with hers. "Cross my heart and hope to die, Hol'. I swear I will be there."

He did exactly that—crossed his heart—like a twelve-year-old. But he didn't know how else to get it through to her other than to use the words they had always used as children in moments of deepest commitment.

"You didn't cross your heart about the boat," Holly said faintly.

Lukas shook his head. "No."

He saw a flickering of something—a softening perhaps—in her gaze as she took a shaky breath. "Well, then, as long as you understand how important it is…" She hesitated, then shrugged. "I guess we're good." A bare hint of a smile tipped one corner of her mouth.

Lukas would have preferred a blinding smile, would have liked her to throw herself into his arms. Fat chance. But it felt like a watershed moment, and now he was the one who needed more convincing. He caught her hand, holding her where she was. "Are we good, Hol'?" His voice was rough.

She blinked. "What?" She shook her head. "I… Yes, of course."

He should have let go of her then. It was all the reassurance he was going to get. But he wanted more. What he wanted from Holly was only partly tangled up with what had happened with Matt. Just as much it was about what Lukas had always—though unadmittedly—felt for her.

And it wasn't just reassurance he was hanging on for

now. It was for the connection, for simply the feeling of Holly's soft skin beneath the roughened calluses on his hand, for the quickened beat of her pulse against his thumb. He could feel the heat rising in him as he looked into her eyes. Any minute she would break contact, move away as she always had. Always—but once…

But she didn't. She stared straight into his gaze. And whatever they had been talking about blew right out the window in the face of the desire he felt for her.

"I want to kiss you." He couldn't stop the words, only knew them for the truth they were. "You know that, don't you?"

Her cheeks went red, and she shook her head rapidly. "No!" She took a quick breath. "Not a good idea."

"Why not?"

"Because…because I said no." She wouldn't look at him.

"Afraid I won't follow through?" Lukas pressed. "Or that I will?"

She jerked away from him. "Stop it!" She crossed the room, put the desk between them.

"There's something between us," he told her. "Don't tell me you don't feel it."

She looked away, shook her head vehemently. "Can't you ever take no for an answer?"

"I can," Lukas said. "But I want to know you mean it."

She flicked a glance back his way. "I mean it." She thrust out her jaw defiantly.

He drew in a slow, careful breath. "Okay." He let the word out just as slowly. He had pushed her before and look where that had got him. Never let it be said that Lukas Antonides didn't learn from his mistakes. "We'll take it slow."

"We won't take it at all," Holly said fiercely.

He raised a brow. That was what she thought. She was back in his life now. He wasn't letting her walk out again without a fight. But he could afford to take his time—for a little while at least. But it went against all of his instincts. He felt like a panther trapped in a birdcage, trying to play by the canary's rules.

Holly apparently took his lack of a verbal reply as acquiescence. She rubbed her hands together as if she were trying to erase the feel of his fingers wrapping hers, then gave him a bright determined smile. "Well, I'm glad we understand each other. About…about everything," she added lamely.

Lukas dipped his head. Let her take it however she wanted.

"Thank you for…understanding about the kids. If you change your mind and decide not to go every week—"

"I won't."

The firmness of his tone must have got through to her. "Well, then, good. I guess," she added awkwardly. "I should go." She was already edging toward the door.

"Why?"

Holly looked confused. "Why what?"

He shoved his hands into his pockets. "Why go?" He glanced at his watch. "It's almost five. We could grab an early dinner."

"I'm going to Althea's for dinner. And Stig's. Have you met Stig?"

Lukas shook his head. "Which one is he?"

"The fourth. And final," Holly said. "I believe in Stig."

"I'll believe it when I see it." Lukas had heard occasional stories about Matt's sister's marital adventures from Matt. Since Matt's death he'd only caught the occasional rumor passed on by his mother. It didn't sound promising.

"You'll believe if you ever meet Stig," Holly assured him. She started toward the door again.

"What time's your dinner?"

"Seven. But I should get there early."

"At five?" Lukas gave her his best skeptical look.

"I need to call my Realtor. She's showing the condo now at this very moment to some lunatic film director." She shook her head. "A location scout saw it last week and thought it might be a good movie set. As if." She gave a small laugh.

"It's got a view."

"I've had a dozen prospective buyers come through since I've put the place on the market, and I haven't had a single offer yet." She looked a bit despondent. "I don't mind if the condo doesn't sell right away, but I'd like an offer I can close on before I leave. The view won't sell it," she said, going back to the current issue. "Lots of places have great views."

"Not this one." Lukas gestured toward the vista outside the tall, narrow windows that gave them a bird's-eye view of other buildings like his own. He was willing her to stick around, to let him get a toe in the door before she vanished again.

Now she came over to look out, too. "You didn't buy it for the view, did you?"

"No. It has great space. You haven't seen it, have you?" Lukas grasped at the straw he should have grabbed in the first place. "Let me show you."

Holly shook her head, moving back toward the door. "I'm going to Althea's."

"Right." Lukas shrugged easily. "And where does she live?"

"The West Seventies."

He nodded. "Yeah, well, it might take you two hours if you walk."

Holly made a face at him. But there was a light in her eyes that had always had the power to stir his blood.

Lukas grinned. "Come on, Hol'. You know you want to see it."

"You want to show it off, you mean."

"Yeah," he said, his grin widening. He breathed easier. "That, too."

"I've never seen anything like it. There's the most amazing art! Stunning textiles, murals, these astonishing fanciful birdcages. Birdcages, if you can believe it!"

Holly knew she was babbling, but her mind still boggled at everything she had seen in Lukas's gallery that afternoon. "And the jewelry…" She gave a shake of her head in near disbelief. "It's absolutely gorgeous. The workmanship is superb. And the opals are the most beautiful I've ever seen."

"You were impressed," Stig said drily, but he grinned at her.

"You could say that." Astonished more like. Partly because she had rarely seen so much appealing art all in one place. But also because it was evident that Lukas had had a very big hand in making it possible.

Of course the *What's New!* article had sung his praises. But articles like that were showpieces intended to paint things in the best light. But Holly's own tour of the gallery, coupled with the enthusiasm of the artists and sculptors she met, told an even more complimentary story.

He'd been eager to show it off, and having seen it now, she could understand why. He was fretting over details even as he showed her around, but she was sure it was going to be a success and she'd told him so.

"You think?" He'd sounded almost doubtful, but genuinely pleased.

"Of course," Holly had said. "The artists are all brilliant. They cover a wide variety of media, and every one of them has some particular gift, some talent that just grabs me."

It was true. She loved the airy textiles and the ornate and elegant birdcages. The wood sculpture was exquisite. The paintings covered the spectrum from primitive to sort of pseudo-impressionist to realistic to dreamy ethereal watercolors. She hadn't been able to decide which she liked best. And the jewelry—the opal rings and necklaces, the brooches and pendants—was simply out of this world.

It wasn't only seeing such wonderful works of art that enchanted her, it was that several of the artists were there, working, right in front of her. Lukas had introduced her to several of them.

"You can talk to them," he'd said. "Comment. Ask questions. Whatever you want. We want to make the art—and the artists—accessible," he'd told her. "We want people to understand the process, the artist's mind."

It was fascinating—and a brilliant marketing move. She could have talked forever with Charlotte, a textile artist who did amazing wall hangings. And the guy who made the birdcages, Sam, was as charming and quirky as he was talented.

He told her all about how he designed the cages, the materials he used, how long it took him to do one, even as he soldered tiny wire flowers in place, making them look like they were growing up the side of a Victorian house. "I have my own ideas," he said. "But I've done a few to order. Want a birdcage? We could have dinner and talk about it," he offered.

"She's busy." And Lukas had hauled her away peremptorily. "Well, you are," he said when she protested. "Having dinner at Althea's, didn't you say?"

"Yes, but I could have continued to talk with him."

"Not now. Come on. There's more to show you."

He took her through all the galleries, including one featuring opal mining. "A little background before we get to the jewelry," he said. There were blown-up photos of the land, the mines, the work he and Skeet had done. She would have liked to look closer, but if she lingered, he took her arm. And Lukas's fingers on her arm were a distraction she didn't need. So when she sensed he was getting impatient, she moved on before he could touch her again.

He showed her the whole building, top to bottom. She had, of course, seen his office when she'd burst into it earlier. But after he took her through the galleries and the studios and workshops, he brought her back upstairs and showed her around his top-floor apartment with its skylights and its twelve-foot ceilings and highly polished oak floors. Her whole condo could have fit in the main living space of his apartment. On one wall, his sister, Martha, had been painting a mural.

"She's not finished," Lukas said. "It's a work in progress. She's adding things as I think of them." So far she had done a panorama of what Holly presumed were significant places and events and people in Lukas's life. There was a New York City skyline, a South Pacific island, the deep reds and ochers of the Australian outback and the blue-and-white houses of Santorini. A man who looked rather like Lukas's friend Skeet was whittling a piece of wood. His parents were dancing at a wedding. Martha herself was with a man Holly guessed was her husband. Three little kids clambered all over them. She spotted the house he'd lived in on the beach in the Hamptons, the facade of the building in which they were standing right now, and a dozen other things—rain forests, old manuscripts, a rough-coated retriever-ish sort of dog—all symbols of Lukas's many interests, of the wide and various enthusiasms of his life.

And, of course, there was a sailboat. Not the one he and Matt had never repaired. This one was whole and skimming through the water. At the helm, looking toward the future, no doubt with his eye out for whatever would catch his fancy next, was a man with sun-streaked, windblown brown hair.

For a moment, Holly couldn't look away.

"When she gets going, there's no stopping her." Lukas came to stand beside her, so close that the sleeve of his shirt brushed her bare arm. The awareness was like a magnetic pull.

Holly moved back so she could get a broader view. So she could step away.

"She's got amazing talent. You should feature her."

"She's already showing at another place in the city. Besides, Martha's not Pacific. Not in any sense of the word," he added with a grin. "You remember Martha?"

"Yes." Martha had, in her way, been as much of a force as her twin. She had always known what she wanted and gone after it. No one in Martha's family was remotely arty or painted murals. Martha did.

"She'd like to see you again," Lukas said. "When she and Theo are in town—they live in Montana—we should get together."

"Sounds like a good idea," Holly said, certain she'd be gone by then. She glanced at her watch. "It's past six thirty. Gotta run."

She had chatted with him all the way down in the elevator, told him again what a great place it was, and, just for good measure, had reiterated that he didn't need to continue showing up for the kids repairing the sailboat as long as he stopped going now.

Lukas nodded. "No worries. I'll be there." And when she'd opened her mouth to protest, he'd said, "I crossed my heart, remember?" Sea-green eyes bored into hers.

"I remember."

"I'll even tell you all about what happened," he said. "Unless you're going to be there yourself."

"No."

"Then I'll tell you at dinner on Saturday."

"I don't—"

"You don't have a date, do you?" he challenged.

Unfortunately no, she didn't. And she wasn't a good enough liar to pretend she did.

He caught sight of a cab and flagged it down, then opened the door for her and shut it again, bending down to lean in the window. "I'll pick you up Saturday at six."

Something she wasn't telling Stig and Althea. God knew what Althea would make of her going out with Lukas.

"We have to go," Althea said to Stig, who was carving the roast.

Stig looked skeptical. "Birdcages?" But then he shrugged. "Why not?"

Althea beamed. "See?" she said to Holly. "Isn't he a dear? And he came with me yesterday and picked out your dress."

"Did he?" Holly tried not to sound as worried as she felt.

Althea nodded happily. "I took him to a couple of boutiques we missed. And he picked a dress." She smiled. "He says it captures the real you."

Which could be ominous. Holly wasn't sure what "real her" Stig was capturing—and how he knew, anyway. They were hardly bosom buddies. She got no clue from the man himself. Stig finished carving and sat back, grinning guilelessly.

"Tell me about it," she suggested.

Stig shook his head. "Wait and see."

"You can see it next week," Althea said, passing her the potatoes. "I can pick it up on Wednesday unless you want to try it on there for alterations?"

"I'll pick it up." She could deal with the alterations herself if Stig had picked something totally outrageous.

"I don't see you as a cupcake," Stig told her.

Well, thank God for that. But Holly didn't have time to worry about it. Over dinner Althea wanted to talk about the wedding reception, and after, when Stig took the dog for a walk, Althea pressed her for more details about Lukas's gallery—and Lukas.

"I didn't think the gallery was open yet, or we'd have gone," she said. "I thought the article said something about the first week in July."

"Yes. Lukas said that, too," Holly agreed. "But it's sort of a gradual process, apparently. Several of the artists are already there, and a lot of their work is already on display. But the hours are still limited."

"But he gave you a tour!" Holly could see the wheels turning in Althea's head.

"He wanted to show it off," Holly said dampeningly. "And it gets him away from going over the finalists for the MacClintock grant, which drives him nuts." He'd told her that.

"I can't see Lukas sitting still for long," Althea agreed.

"He's doing a lot of the actual carpentry on the apartments." For all that he disparaged his contribution, Holly understood that he'd done a lot of the finish work as well as what he'd described as "grunt stuff."

"I'll bet he looks good in a tool belt."

Holly was quite sure he did, too, and felt her face warm at the thought. Determinedly ignoring it, she talked about the gallery opening instead.

"He's waiting on the gallery manager," she said. "She's coming from Sydney next week. I gather she's very good at this sort of thing. Can do it with one hand tied behind her back—or from the other side of the world. But he wants her here before they officially open. So that's why they're waiting for the grand opening."

"You're going, of course," Althea said as she loaded the dishwasher. It wasn't a question.

"I might be back out at my mother's by then."

Althea looked up, startled. "At your mother's? Why?"

"I'm hoping the condo sells. If it does…I have to go somewhere." She took a swallow of the wine Stig had poured for her before they cleared the table. "I'm just doing wishful thinking here."

"You won't have to move in three weeks," Althea protested. "You haven't even sold it yet, have you?"

"No." She swirled the wine in her glass, staring at it moodily. "I'm just hoping I will. I don't want to have to deal with it long distance—particularly not 'out of the country' long distance. I should have put it on the market before now." Her brother, Greg, had told her at Christmastime to put it on the market then. But Holly hadn't been ready then. She'd only just made the decision to go. "I am going to have to get a storage locker somewhere soon anyway."

Althea finished putting the last dishes in, then turned the dishwasher on. Drying her hands, she turned to Holly. "It still seems insane to me. Giving up everything. Going halfway round the world."

It wasn't the first time they'd had this chat. Holly said, "I'm sure."

And not just for all the reasons she'd had before.

Now she also needed to put a world between herself and Lukas Antonides.

She might not know what she wanted out of the rest of her life, but it was perfectly clear what Lukas wanted—a roll in the hay or the urban equivalent thereof.

His "I want to kiss you" in that sexy sandpaper voice had sent shivers right down from her neck to her toes. Still did.

He hadn't done it, but he hadn't been joking. And if he had kissed her, he wouldn't have stopped there. When Lukas wanted something, he was single-minded. If he decided he wanted Holly, he would do his damnedest to get her into bed.

But scariest of all was Holly's fear that she might not stop him.

He waited for the other shoe to drop.

Ever since he'd helped Holly into the cab, Lukas had expected a phone call saying that something had come up, that she wouldn't be able to have dinner with him on Saturday night after all.

He deliberately worked with power tools all evening so he wouldn't hear the phone when it rang. But when he checked his voice mail before he went to bed that night, there was no message from Holly.

There were seven others, including one from Jenn, the office manager who was supposed to be arriving Monday.

"Ah, Luke," she'd said, her normal Aussie drawl powered by excitement. "Really sorry, but I can't come! Bryan's popped the question! Who knew?"

Lukas ground his teeth. Who indeed? And where the

hell was he going to find a gallery manager at this late date? He wanted to tear his hair out.

The other six messages were from various family members, all inviting him to come out to his parents' place in the Hamptons the weekend after next.

"I miss you," his grandmother had said. "Why did you come back to New York if you don't come out here?"

"Theo and the kids and I will be at the folks' this weekend," Martha had said. "You know you want to see us."

"Week from Saturday, Mom and Dad's. Be there," Cristina had commanded.

Only his mother had been unable to conceal the real agenda. "The Panathakoses will be here all week," she'd said. "You remember their beautiful daughter, Angelika? She's looking forward to seeing you again."

Lukas had groaned. But he'd taken heart, too. At least none of the messages was from Holly.

Still, that left Friday—and all day Saturday—for her to change her mind, to come up with some excuse that he would have to argue with before he got to see her again. She didn't call on Friday—and he was in the office all day, trying to round up a new gallery manager and finishing a preliminary run-through of the final group of potential grant recipients.

It felt like the longest day in history as he kept himself almost tied to his chair, sensing Skeet gazing down the back of his neck. But at the end of the day he had a stack of twenty finalists from which to make his three choices. He also had a list of half a dozen possible gallery manager candidates that Sera must have pulled out of a hat—and he knew for a fact that Holly hadn't tried to reach him. There was no message on his phone, and Sera hadn't heard from her, either.

He was whistling when he went to the boatyard Saturday morning. The kids were delighted to see him, and he had to admit Holly was right: they had been counting on him being there.

That time passed quickly, but the afternoon dragged. He needed to talk to both his cousin Alex and to the contractor before he did more on the apartment where he was working. He'd done enough grant proposals to fry his brain permanently. And he still had four hours until he could legitimately appear on Holly's doorstep.

So he went over to Elias and Tallie's place for distraction.

"I thought you were supposed to choose the winners yourself," Tallie chided when he appeared in her kitchen and dropped into a chair and tossed a pile of grant proposals on the table in front of him.

"Yes. And I will. But I don't entirely trust myself," he admitted. He poked a finger at the stack of applications. "These are, in my estimation, the most promising of the lot. But I still want to bang some heads against the wall and say, 'Get on with it. You don't need a grant to get off your butt and make a change.'"

Tallie laughed. "Probably not what your friend had in mind."

"He should have," Lukas muttered. "But—" he raked a hand through his hair "—you're right. He expected me to be supportive." And if his lips twisted on the last word, well, there was just so far he could make himself go. "Anyway, I thought maybe you could give me your opinion. I promise I'll make the final decision," he added quickly.

Sounds of boys shouting and scuffling their way down the stairs interrupted them. Tallie glanced toward the stairs and winced at Digger's sudden bellow. "Not sure when I'll have time. Elias took a prospective client out for a sail today. So it's just me and the heathens."

"I'll take 'em to the park," Lukas said.

"You must be desperate. Be my guest." Tallie made shooing movements toward the door with her hands.

"Thea, too?" Lukas looked warily at his niece, who was banging her spoon on the kitchen table. She was somewhere on the not-quite-civilized side of three, but a force in her own right—as only a girl with three older brothers could be.

"No. She still needs a nap. And she might even get one with the boys gone. Can you keep them away until four?" she asked hopefully.

"My pleasure," Lukas assured her.

"Thank you. I should be doing it for you anyway," Tallie added. "I owe you."

Lukas's raised his brows. "You do?" He didn't remember doing her any favors recently.

"For what I said when you brought your friend—Holly—over last weekend. Calling her Grace." Even now the color flushed Tallie's cheeks.

Lukas's mouth twisted. "It worked out. Gave me a reason to explain who Grace is—and isn't—in my life."

"Is it serious? You and Holly?"

Lukas grimaced. "Nothing to be serious about."

"Really? I thought you looked interested. You certainly turned red when I called her Grace!"

Lukas shrugged. He had denied it for so long that it had become part of who he was—the guy who wasn't interested in Holly. But now he said cautiously, "I could be. Maybe."

Tallie laughed. "Well, don't bowl her over with your enthusiasm."

The boys bounced into the kitchen just then so he didn't reply. He didn't know what he'd have said anyway. What was there to say?

"Uncle Lukas is going to take you to the park," she told the boys.

Instantly, the stampede was on. Tallie smiled at him. "Go to the park," she commanded. "Have a good time. The boys will keep you busy. You won't have time to answer your phone."

Lukas gathered up bats and balls, baseball gloves, a football and a soccer ball, then chivvied Garrett, Nick and Digger out the door.

"Don't let them drive you nuts." Tallie fixed him with a hard look.

Lukas just grinned. "They're fine." The noise and bounce of little boys was easy to handle. It was the rest of his life—well, what he felt about Holly and what she felt about him—that threatened his sanity. He dropped his mobile phone on the kitchen counter.

"What's this?" Tallie said.

"I don't want any interruptions."

Tallie looked doubtful, but he didn't offer any other explanation—especially not the real one: that he didn't want a phone call from Holly telling him she had changed her mind.

But he wasn't entirely surprised when he brought them back shortly after four that she had left a message on his voice mail.

Lukas waited until he was back in his SUV to listen to it. "Sorry to leave it so late." Holly sounded slightly breathless and just a bit frazzled. "But I can't go to dinner. I've sold the condo and I have to clear things out. Maybe we can do it another time…like in a couple of years when I get back." There was a light strained laugh. "Anyway, thanks for the invitation. See you someday. Maybe. Love your gallery." And then there was a click.

See you someday. Maybe.

Another end—before it really began.

No. Not someday. Not maybe. There was something between them—always had been. For years they hadn't allowed themselves to discover what it might become. Maybe nothing. He had to admit that. Maybe he'd just been focusing on her because, in a sense, she was the one who'd got away.

Girls had normally flocked to him. *It's disgusting*, Martha said, *The way you practically have to beat them off with a stick. Can't any girl say no to you?*

One had. One did.

Maybe if he got her to say yes—and want him, mind, body and soul—that would be enough. Maybe, though, he was as guilty as Skeet of not going after what he thought he wanted. Did he want a foundation to help him do it?

Hell, no.

And what kind of excuse was selling her condo? It didn't mean she had to stop eating.

At least she loved his gallery.

You had to start somewhere.

The unexpected chime of the doorbell reached Holly even deep within the bedroom closet. She ignored it, swiped a hand across her damp brow and plunged even deeper into the mess. She had to get through it, pack what she intended to keep, and donate the rest to the charity shop on Monday. Then she needed to start on the books. God, the books! They were going to be far worse than the closet.

The doorbell rang again. Longer this time. Louder.

Not really. But if a doorbell could sound determined, this one did.

Holly sighed and muttered under her breath. There was only one person who rang her doorbell with that singular determination—Deb from across the hall, wanting to

borrow a cup of sugar, a teaspoon of horseradish, a bag
of mixed greens.

Holly was Deb's go-to alternative to the grocery store
when she couldn't be bothered. And she didn't give up.

The bell went again—even longer and more persistent
than the last time. Clearly, Deb wasn't going away. Instead,
she was leaning on the bell.

Holly sighed and extricated herself from the depths
of the closet and, irritation building, pasted on a long-
suffering smile as she stalked to the door and jerked it
open.

"What now? I've packed—" Her voice died.

It wasn't Deb. It was Lukas.

Clad in faded jeans and a pale blue button-down shirt,
his jaw freshly shaved and a lock of sun-tipped hair drift-
ing over his forehead, Lukas Antonides looked crisp and
casual, and as drop-dead gorgeous as a Greek god.

Holly looked—and felt—like a warmed-over stew of
irritation and exhaustion. "I told you I couldn't go out.
Don't tell me you didn't get the message."

"I got your message."

And didn't pay any attention, apparently, because he
walked straight past her into the chaos that was her living room.

Holly didn't have the strength to deal with him and
the rest of her life. "Lukas! I said no. I have work to do!"

"Yeah. You're moving. In August, you said."

"Tuesday."

"What?" He stared at her.

"I sold the condo. And I have to be out by Tuesday."

Now Lukas's brows really did shoot up. "Tuesday? As
in three days—" she could see him doing a quick mental
calculation "—three days from now?"

"Not even." Holly glanced at her watch. "Sixty-one

hours and thirty-two minutes from now. That's when we close."

"That's crazy. Doesn't make sense. No one does that."

"Fraser Holcomb does."

"Fraser Holcomb? *The* Fraser Holcomb?" So Lukas had heard of the hotshot young film director. Holly hadn't. She wasn't a big film buff.

"The very one." She followed Lukas back into the living room where stacks of too much stuff and too few boxes covered every surface. "I told you some location scout came and looked at the place."

Lukas waved a hand in the direction of Manhattan. "He liked what he saw?"

"Seems he did." Which was something of an understatement. Amber the Realtor had called her Friday afternoon and squealed, "He loved it! He thinks it's perfect!"

Holly hadn't believed her. It was too preposterous. It still felt preposterous even though she now had it in writing. "He made a cash offer yesterday morning. I told Amber I didn't have anyplace to go. She told him, and he said, 'She can rent a place until August for a hundred thousand dollars, can't she?'" She swallowed. "He offered me an extra hundred grand above the asking price for immediate occupancy."

Lukas whistled silently.

Holly let out a ragged breath. "I said yes. Amber would have killed me if I hadn't. And it really was too good to pass up," she admitted. "But now I'm panicking. I need to get packed up. Find a storage facility." She shook her head. "So I really can't…"

Lukas looked around for just a moment, taking it all in, then looked back at her. "Where do you want me to start?"

Holly goggled at him. "What? No! You don't have to do anything! I was just trying to explain why I can't—"

"I understand, but it's obvious you can't do this all yourself. You were trying to do it all yourself, weren't you?" His gaze was mildly accusing.

"It's my condo. My life."

"And since Matt died you don't count on anyone."

She flinched at his perception. "That's right," she said stubbornly.

"How's that working for you?" He said it gently, making Holly sigh in recognition of how badly it was working.

"I should hire a mover."

"No. You've got me."

The mulish look on his face said arguing was going to get her nowhere, and that she would be wasting precious time trying to change his mind. She shrugged. "Fine. Start boxing." She pointed toward the piles of stuff she'd hauled out of the closet, then she realized the flaw in the plan. "I don't have enough boxes."

"I do."

She frowned. "You?"

But he was digging his cell phone out of his pocket as he spoke. "Who just moved in?" he reminded her. "And we've got all that art we've just uncrated."

"Oh!" She actually felt a stab of relief. "Yes, of course."

He started punching in a number, then stopped to look at her. "Do you have an apartment to go to?"

"I'll go out to my mom's. I just need to get hold of her and tell her. She's not in the country now. She's in Scotland on a tour. I've been trying to reach her." Unsuccessfully, as it happened. She hadn't really planned to move in on her mother so early. A week, she'd thought. Maybe two right before she left. She hadn't planned on six weeks. "If I can't get hold of my mom, I can find a suite at the Plaza." She put all the bravado she could muster into her grin.

"And your stuff?" Lukas tilted his head.

She sucked in a breath. "A storage unit. I've called a few places."

"Are you wedded to the storage unit idea?"

"Why?"

"You could store your stuff at my place."

She shook her head. "No, I couldn't. I don't want to take advantage! I—"

"I suppose you could say no," Lukas said mildly. "Pay through the nose for some little storage unit where your stuff will bake all summer and freeze all winter."

"And of course it wouldn't at your place." Holly knew when she was being led down the primrose path.

"It wouldn't. I heat my building in winter, I air-condition in summer." He smiled.

Feeling virtual rope tightening around her ankles, Holly waited for him to go in for the kill. But he didn't say another word. He just waited, letting her stew. Letting her realize she was being foolish by saying no to his suggestion.

"I'm paying you," she said at last, feeling ungracious and guilty at the same time she felt a prickle of relief knowing that she wouldn't have to just take the first place she found without doing her homework—homework she'd intended to do and now didn't have time for.

"If you want." Lukas shrugged, but he didn't argue with her. "I thought I might pay you," he added after a moment.

Holly glanced at him sharply. "What on earth for?"

"Being my gallery manager until I can hire a full-time permanent one."

She stared, astonished. "Your…gallery manager? Don't be ridiculous. I don't know anything about managing a gallery."

"You can manage a classroom of sixth graders," he said as if that was all it required. "And you always kept a handle on Matt and me. Kept us focused. Kept me focused," he amended with a twist of his lips. "Matt was always focused."

"Not always," Holly murmured. He was perpetually being led astray by Lukas's next scheme or great idea. But she didn't say that. "You don't want me to manage your gallery," she said firmly. "You're just being kind."

Lukas looked genuinely astonished. "When have you ever known me to be kind?"

There was a sudden silence. Holly's instinct was to say she hadn't. But that wasn't entirely true. That night on his dad's sailboat, to her way of thinking, he had not been kind at all, but the day after, she had expected him to tell Matt what had happened—and he hadn't.

Instead, he had walked out of their lives.

"You can be," she allowed.

"Well, I'm not now. I'm looking out for my own interests, believe me. I need a gallery manager. Jenn isn't coming. And the chances of me finding someone like her are not great. It's going to take a while. I don't want to grab someone off the street."

"Like me," Holly pointed out.

"I want to take my time and do it right," Lukas went on just as if she hadn't said a word. "So I'm asking you to do it until you leave. Six weeks max. Long enough to give me a chance to gather a reasonable pool of candidates and find the right one—and in the meantime you have a place to stay. I showed you the apartment I'd finished for the manager," he reminded her. "You're welcome to it. Part of the pay. You can store your stuff there all the time you're gone. I've got a lot of space. And I know you can do the bare essentials that need to be done."

"What bare essentials?"

"People skills mostly. You've got 'em. I've seen you

with people. You charm them. You calm them. You make them do the right thing. You made *me* do the right thing."

"I've never made you do anything!"

"Yes, Hol', you did."

Then he just rocked on his heels and looked at her expectantly. As if he knew what she'd decide, and he didn't even have to argue his case.

Of course she could say no. It would be the wise thing to do.

Taking Lukas up on his offer was crazy. Reckless. Especially when deep down she'd wanted him for years. And past experience proved that she hadn't been able to resist him.

How was she going to move into his building for six weeks and keep her distance, be his business manager and, in August, walk away without ever a taste of forbidden fruit?

She wasn't. It was as simple as that.

Holly was tired of being wise, of being sensible and responsible. She had chosen wisdom and responsibility and a slow hearth fire of love when she'd married Matt.

And look where that had got her.

No, that wasn't fair. She'd loved Matt. She could never regret that love, those years. But all the memories in the world didn't make her less lonely every night. They didn't keep her warm. And it wasn't enough to date Paul anymore. Paul was a place marker. Nothing more.

And Holly wanted more.

Somewhere deep inside her—or maybe not so deep inside her—she had felt that desire quickening to life. Maybe it had started last fall when she'd realized how hollow and empty her life had become. Maybe her move toward the Peace Corps was part of it, an attempt to help her find herself again.

Or maybe it was Lukas's gallery. There was an energy there that had spoken to her. She had felt it in the paintings, in the sculptures and textiles. She had spotted it in the fire of the opals set in silver. She had caught glimpses of it in some large photos that weren't part of the gallery offerings at all. They were snapshots really—of the land, of the mines, of Lukas and an old man she was sure had to be his friend Skeet. She'd wanted to look more closely at them, but Lukas hadn't given her a chance. He had urged her on to the next room to other displays.

Or maybe it was Lukas himself.

For the first time she faced squarely the temptation that was Lukas Antonides. A temptation she'd resisted—wisely—for years.

He didn't want what she wanted.

He didn't want commitment, permanence, family—the things she and Matt had valued. Lukas was a man of drive and enthusiasms, not of constants. He spearheaded efforts. He wasn't there for the follow-through.

But sometimes there was no follow-through.

Sometimes the man you had vowed to love and share a lifetime with wasn't there anymore. Sometimes all your hopes and dreams were dashed.

What then?

She would never find again what she'd had with Matt. It hadn't been perfect—neither of them had been perfect—but it was theirs.

And now it was gone. Playing it safe and responsible hadn't guaranteed a lifetime of happiness.

So why not take a risk?

She wasn't a child any longer. She wasn't a skittish, nervy adolescent.

She'd felt the pull of Lukas Antonides for most of her

life. He didn't want what she wanted in the long run. But life wasn't only about the long run, she'd learned.

Six weeks ought to be long enough for both of them. In six weeks she would go off to the South Pacific and put the past behind her.

In the meantime, she'd take it one step at a time. One word at a time.

She said, "Yes."

CHAPTER SEVEN

Yes?

Lukas had been staring out at the Manhattan skyline telling himself to shut up, not to give in to pressuring her, not—for once—to push. At least not until she said no, at which point he was prepared to argue with her again.

And then she said…yes?

His gaze whipped around, and he stared straight at her. He expected her to be looking in the other direction—out the window, at the floor, anywhere but at him. He expected her to say, *Er, I mean, no.*

But Holly was looking straight into his eyes, not averting her gaze at all. Staring resolutely at him.

Like a deer caught in headlights. Well, maybe. But she didn't look precisely stunned. She looked intense, committed. Alive.

Lukas didn't let himself wonder what had prompted her. He didn't even know what had prompted him to make the offer. As always, he had responded to the circumstances. And, let's face it, he had done what he'd wanted to do. How could he not want her close?

So he'd jumped right out of the frying pan and into the fire. It wasn't enough to tempt himself by accidental-on-purpose meetings and invitations to dinner. Now he had drawn her into his building, his work, his life.

He would see her every day. They'd work together. Talk together. No doubt argue together. And then what?

Lukas had never done relationships. Not real, long-term, committed relationships—except with people to whom he was related by blood or family ties. He wasn't sure he knew how. Or if he wanted to.

Cold feet, anyone? he jeered at himself silently.

But his feet didn't feel cold at the moment. They felt eager, alive, ready to run a marathon. *Hold that thought*, he counseled himself.

He grinned at her. "Terrific. Welcome aboard." He punched in a number on his mobile phone.

Charlotte, the textile artist, the one whose work Holly had particularly admired, answered at once.

"Rustle up as many of the bunch as you can," he told her. "We need lots of hands. And bring all the boxes and crates you can find. We're going to move in our new gallery manager."

And just like that, Lukas sorted out her life.

One minute Holly was suffocating in dust and clutter and far too many decisions—about what to keep and what to toss and where to put anything she hung on to—and the next, Lukas had taken over.

It was like the first time she'd gone white-water kayaking. She had been moving down a stream nice and easy—everything under control. And then she'd spied rapids ahead and instinctively began sculling backward, apprehensive, trying to size things up, to get a bead on a through-line, to keep control the way Matt had told her to.

Then all her planning, all her care vanished as she felt the surge of the water beneath her, lifting and pulling the kayak past the point of no return. The current simply swept her up in its power and carried her into the rapids.

Then all she could do was pray—and hang on to the paddle for dear life.

Exactly the way she was doing now. Minus the paddle.

Lukas Antonides in action was a class-four set of whitewater rapids. Within an hour half a dozen of the artists, sculptors and jewelry makers she'd met turned up on her doorstep with boxes and crates galore.

"What goes? What stays? Tell us what to do," Sam, the birdcage maker, said.

"We're experts at packing," Charlotte told her. "I'm so glad you're going to work with us."

The other three, Geoff and Paul and Teresa, nodded in agreement.

"Where's the boss?" Geoff asked, looking around with a grin.

"I'm the boss," Holly said firmly and wished she actually sounded like it. She still felt dizzy. "Lukas went to get pizza and beer."

By the time he got back, Holly and her helpers had blitzed their way through the kitchen and the hall closet. It was easier, she found, to have the others there, not just for the help, but for the distance their involvement gave her.

It was less painful to step back and say yes to this and no to that when Charlotte or Geoff held up something than it was to handle each piece herself and be caught by indecision or carried away by memories.

By the time Lukas got back, they'd cleared the kitchen and bathroom entirely. After a brief pause for sustenance, he herded the guys into her bedroom to begin dismantling the bed and carrying the dressers down to the truck.

"Hey, wait! I have to sleep somewhere," Holly protested.

"In your new apartment." Lukas was collapsing the bed frame as he spoke. "You're moving. Remember?"

Holly swallowed. She'd just assumed she'd have until Tuesday to get used to the idea. Lukas, as usual, had other plans.

"What about this tablecloth?" Teresa appeared in the doorway. "Save or sell?"

So while Lukas and the other guys got on with dismantling her life, Holly went back to the living room and made another decision.

She made hundreds before they were done. But by ten o'clock all the furniture had been ferried to the gallery building, and stacks of boxes containing things she knew she wasn't keeping stood in the middle of the otherwise empty bedroom. And another stack of boxes with the things she was storing at Lukas's were in the living room. The cupboards were empty. The bookshelves were bare.

Now everyone had gone back to the gallery to unload the truck except Holly—and Lukas. He was labeling the boxes in the bedroom. She had finished with the last box in the living room and, at a loose end, moved restlessly around the room. The lights of Manhattan gleamed like bright patterns of stars across the river. They looked familiar, unlike the mostly empty room in which she stood. She stared at them, remembering the first night she and Matt had spent in the condo. They'd sat up all night, huddled together under a blanket on the sofa, just marveling at the view.

"Ours," Matt had said and turned his head to kiss her. "We're going to make wonderful memories here."

And they had, too, Holly thought, swallowing around the tightness in her throat. Just not enough of them.

And now she didn't belong here anymore. There was nothing left.

She looked around, wondering where Lukas had got to. She cocked her head, listening closely, and realized she could hear water running in the back of the apartment. There were muffled sounds and occasional clattering noises punctuating the sound of the water. Curious, Holly followed the sounds down the hall and into the bathroom. The door was open. Lukas was on his knees, scrubbing the grout around the edge of the shower.

"You don't have to do that!"

He sat back on his heels and looked around at her, then shrugged. "Okay." But he made no move to get up.

"I can clean it myself," she protested.

"Yeah." He straightened slowly and stood, eyeing her speculatively, and Holly began to realize what he was doing. Lukas wasn't on his knees in the bathroom with an old toothbrush in his hand because he was desperate to clean grout or because he thought she couldn't do it herself. He had been giving her space and time of her own.

She took a breath and smiled—a little wanly perhaps, but it was still a smile. "Thank you."

Lukas's gaze flicked over her. "You okay?"

"Yes." Then, more firmly, "I'm fine. I will be fine."

"Of course you will be," he agreed. "Are you ready to go?"

She tilted her head, considering. "Unless you want to scrub the rest of the grout?"

He grinned, getting to his feet. "I believe Fraser Holcomb can do the rest."

He was an idiot.

His own worst enemy.

The guy least likely to get laid on the planet.

All of the above.

He now had temptation on his doorstep 24/7—and it was his own damn fault.

Lukas sprawled on his bed, staring up at the skylight, and wondered when the hell he was going to get a clue.

Not only had he pushed his way in when she had clearly left a message telling him no, he'd got the bright idea of hiring her to be his gallery manager, then moved her into the manager's apartment where she would be right there in his building for the next six weeks. Underfoot.

Then, heaven help him, he'd shared a glass of wine with her and had the unfortunate realization that she was shattered from leaving the last home she'd shared with Matt, whereupon he had somewhere—somehow!—discovered the scruples to tell her good-night, turn his back and walk out the door!

God.

Lukas thrust his fingers through his hair and flung himself over onto his stomach. It didn't help. In fact, it was worse. It brought his arousal into direct contact with the friction of the bedclothes and made him more desperate than ever.

He either needed the brains to recognize how far gone he was on Holly—and how far she wasn't gone on him—and so keep her at a distance instead of tormenting himself with the knowledge that she was sound asleep in her bed four floors below him, or he needed to be unscrupulous enough to pursue a woman who was still in love with another man.

But this—having her right under his nose every day and still keeping his hands off—was likely going to kill him.

He rolled over to the other side, then, irritably, flipped onto his back.

He'd bet Holly wasn't tossing and turning. She'd looked completely spent by the time they'd got her furniture where she wanted it and had made up her bed.

The others had helped bring things up, but then Holly

had thanked them profusely and sent them away, saying they'd done enough. She'd tried to send him away, too. But he'd had to offer to help.

He could hardly insist she move in, then abandon her the minute she got there. He probably should have. Being there with her, in the intimacy of her bedroom—even one primarily filled with boxes—hell, it was like having her on his dad's sailboat all over again.

She'd dug out a pair of soft, pale blue sheets and they'd stood on either side of the bed, spreading them and straightening them. And it was all Lukas could do not to make some comment about spending the night in them. God knew he wanted to.

But he'd seen her hollow-eyed exhaustion, and he'd witnessed the emptiness in her expression as the condo had stopped being her home and had become just a holding space for pieces of what had once been her life with Matt.

He could get her out of the condo, but he couldn't intrude on her memories. She deserved to have them, to remember the man she'd loved and lost. She had been silent on the drive across the bridge into Manhattan. He'd seen her fingers twist in her lap, and he'd wondered what he was doing bringing her here.

Certainly not what he'd hoped in the mad moments he'd pushed for her to come. It had seemed like a perfect opportunity to get her where he could spend time with her, get to know her again—without being the odd man out this time. Charm her off her feet. Go to bed with her.

But she hadn't even been able to look at him while they were putting sheets on her bed. And he'd been ready to cut his losses and head out the door when she'd said quickly, "I have a bottle of wine. We should drink a toast to my new life."

Anyone less likely to be embracing a new life than the

Holly who'd smiled tremulously at him would have been hard to imagine. Her face was pale, her eyes deep-sunken. She looked as if she was going to shatter any second.

But maybe a glass of wine would settle her, make her sleep. And apparently he was a glutton for punishment, because Lukas had found himself nodding. "Sounds good."

She'd found the wine without too much trouble, and even came up with a corkscrew to open it with. "Charlotte labeled the kitchen boxes very thoroughly," she'd said with a laugh.

But she'd fumbled with the corkscrew and muttered in frustration. So Lukas had taken it from her and done it himself. "Got glasses?"

She'd rooted in another box and produced a pair. He'd poured, then set the bottle down and raised his glass to her. And Holly had looked at him with her eyes wide and terrified looking.

Lukas didn't speak. He didn't know what to say that wouldn't make things worse. Then at last Holly smiled, a small, twisted smile. "To the future."

It sounded as if she was expecting one unmitigated disaster after another. But as long as she didn't say so, Lukas could drink to that.

He clinked his glass to hers. "To the future."

She had taken a sip, then followed it with something close to a gulp, after which she had coughed herself silly. Lukas had taken her glass and set it on the counter, then didn't know what to do with his hands. Patting her on the back—touching her at all—was out of the question.

She'd laughed, a little desperately to his ears. "God," she'd muttered. "I'm hopeless."

Lukas had shaken his head. "No. You just need a good night's sleep," he added. "Everything will be all right in the morning."

Of course it wouldn't. It was just one of those platitudes his mother used to tell him. "Let's hope so," she'd said.

"Right. I'll go. Let you get some sleep." He gulped down the rest of his wine and turned for the door.

Holly followed him. "Thank you, Lukas."

Her voice sounded breathless and achingly sexy, and he needed to get out of there before he did something he'd regret. He gave her a wave of his hand without even turning around. "G'night."

Then he had shut the door behind him with a solid thunk.

So he hoped to God she was sleeping now. She'd been tired enough. As for him—well, no rest for the wicked. Another of his mother's platitudes. And one better suited for the occasion.

From outside Lukas heard the wail of a siren, reminding him that there were people with greater problems than his. The clock on his dresser read 2:42 a.m. He wasn't going to sleep.

He wanted to get up and go knock down a wall, get rid of some of the tension. But there were no walls that needed knocking down. He groaned and rolled over again.

And that was when he heard the knock.

Knock? There was no one in the building but him.

And Holly.

Holly was knocking on his door? He half vaulted out of the bed before he dropped back again, breathing hard.

Suppose it was Holly. Suppose she needed him to fix the thermostat or maybe the refrigerator wasn't working. Suppose she was afraid of the dark in a new place and wanted him to sit with her until dawn.

Did she trust him enough to do any of those things in the middle of the night?

Did he trust himself? Lukas scrubbed his hands down

his face. Trust himself? Ha. He slumped back against the pillows and assured himself that he was hearing things. Tormenting himself with imaginary knocks from a woman who, God help him, wasn't imaginary at all.

And then he heard it again. A little louder.

Definitely not imaginary.

Lukas shoved himself up and yanked on a pair of jeans, the better to disguise the lingering evidence of arousal. Then he put his game face on and padded barefoot to the door.

A glimpse through the security viewer confirmed his worst fears—Holly, hair mussed, in shorts and an oversize T-shirt, shifted from one foot to the other, raised her hand to knock again, then let it drop to her side, fingers twisting. Once more she half raised it, then cradled it in her other hand, turned and started to walk away.

He didn't even hesitate. Lukas jerked open the door. "What's wrong?"

She spun back to face him, eyes wide, her mouth opening in a soundless O as she met his gaze. He saw her throat work once, then again.

"What's wrong, Holly?" he asked again, doing his best to keep his voice calm, steady, the exact opposite of his hammering heart. "What do you need?"

She dragged in a breath, then straightened her shoulders. Her gaze never left his. "You."

Lukas hadn't heard right. He gave a shake of his head. "What?"

"That's right, Lukas. Make me repeat it." Her mouth twisted. "You, damn it. You."

As she came back toward him, her breasts jiggling beneath the soft cotton of her shirt, Lukas caught his breath. She wasn't wearing a bra. He remembered what it was like to slide his hands under her shirt, to stroke her there.

His fingers curled into fists. He dragged his gaze upward, which turned out to be just as bad. She had devilishly kissable lips.

"For what?" his voice rasped. Because if this had to do with fixing a light or some other damn household emergency, he was going to shoot himself.

"What do you think?" She stopped barely a foot from him, looking up into his eyes, hers challenging him the way she always had as a kid. He didn't think of her as a kid now. He hadn't thought of her as a kid for years. All he really thought was how much he wanted to take that extra step, haul her into his arms and feel those soft breasts against his bare chest, press the fierceness of his desire hard against her.

"Holly." He shut his eyes and ground his teeth in frustration.

"Mmm?" Why the hell did her voice sound almost like a purr? Was that her breath he felt against his collarbone?

"Holly!" he protested, strangling on her name.

Her hand came up, went flat against his chest and pushed. He took a step back into his apartment. Holly followed.

"Holly," he warned. "Don't start something you're not going to finish."

"I intend to finish." She sounded almost fierce and she was still close enough that he felt her breath on his bare chest. "Why did you ask me to move in?"

He shrugged. "Why not? I've got space. I need a gallery manager. I figured you could do that."

"I have no clue how to manage a gallery."

"Then why did you take the job?" he demanded. She wasn't the only one who could push. Two could play this game, damn it.

"Because it gave me an excuse." Holly edged even

closer. "We want an excuse, don't we, to get what we really want?" Her voice was soft, enticing, and just a little edgy.

Lukas's breath caught in his chest. Her eyes were deep pools of midnight, so deep he felt he could fall straight into them. "What do you mean, what we really want?" he said roughly. Since when had they ever wanted the same thing?

"I told you what I want." He could hear his heart beat in his chest. "You."

There was no doubt what she was talking about now. Bed. That was what she was talking about. Sex. Lukas frowned.

"Don't you act like you don't want me, Lukas Antonides! Don't you dare try to pretend you were just doing me a favor, giving me a roof over my head!" She poked a fierce finger into his chest. "Because that isn't what this is about. Is it?"

Lukas's jaw tightened. "So, you just want to go to bed? Have sex? And then what?"

Holly shrugged "I don't know. If it's good, maybe we could do it again?" She looked almost hopeful.

And Lukas almost laughed. It would be good. He had no doubt about that. But he still didn't move. "Say we do," he said almost conversationally, which was a far cry from the way his body was clamoring to do just that, "go to bed. Have sex. More than once," he clarified. "What then? What's the point?"

Holly's eyes went wide. "What's the point? It's sex, for heaven's sake! That *is* the point! We go to bed—multiple times, if necessary—and we get it out of our systems. Once and for all!"

"Get it out of our systems? Sex?" He stared at her.

"Not sex," Holly said hotly. "Each other!"

Not likely, Lukas thought. If he could have got Holly out of his system, he'd have done it years ago.

"You won't even have to break up with me," she went on cheerfully. "It's perfect. We can have a six-week affair. Then we go our separate ways. I head off for the far side of the world, and you do whatever you're planning to do next. Simple. See?"

Lukas saw. He thought she was completely out of her flaming mind. It made him furious at the same time it made him desperate.

"You think that'll work?" Pardon his skepticism.

"Of course it will work."

If she were taller, she would have been nose to nose with him now. As it was her breasts were within a millimeter of touching his bare chest. He caught a whiff of citrus scent, enticing him further.

He lifted a hand and touched her cheek, ran his finger down it to linger at the point of her chin. She held herself absolutely still, didn't even seem to be breathing. He wanted her breathing. Panting. Eager. Desperate for him.

He bent his head just as Holly lifted her hands and laid both against his chest.

It was like being branded. Lukas's jaw tightened. Everything else did, too. His nipples beaded under the touch of her palms. She rubbed them over him experimentally. He swallowed a groan and lowered his mouth to hers.

CHAPTER EIGHT

THE KISS BEGAN SLOWLY, almost gently, echoing the kiss of long ago, as if Lukas were leashing his passion, keeping everything under tight control.

Then his tongue touched hers. And Holly could taste him on her lips. Instinctively, hers parted to give him entrance, wanting more. The kiss became harder, more urgent, almost desperate.

It felt exactly the way she felt—the way she had been trying *not* to feel for so long that it was a relief to not have to try to resist. She wanted what Lukas wanted—to touch, to taste. More than taste—to devour.

Of their own volition, her hands slid up the hair-roughened muscular expanse of his chest. She felt tiny nubs beneath her fingers, tweaked them and heard him groan. Holly swallowed his groan, darting her tongue between his lips to touch his teeth even as his tangled with hers. His hands, hard and warm and calloused, slid beneath her T-shirt, drawing her even closer, claiming her.

It wouldn't last, Holly knew that. It was desire. Lust. Passion. It was sex, just as Lukas had said. And it would run its course. It wasn't love. For it to be love, it had to be mutual. It had to knit together two people, create a relationship, make them better and stronger together than they were apart. They had to want that.

Lukas didn't. He'd made it clear more than once.

Love was what she'd had with Matt—a sense of completeness that they had shared. A bedrock of enduring love that worlds—galaxies—could be built on.

This was a shooting star.

But what was wrong with a shooting star? It was short and sweet and stunningly beautiful. And when it burned out, as Holly knew it would, it couldn't possibly hurt more than losing Matt had. And she would have the memory of Lukas. She would never have to wonder.

And wasn't that better than no star at all?

She assured herself it was. And she promised herself she wouldn't get burned. It was just pointless to keep denying the attraction. Everything she'd believed in when she'd married Matt hadn't prevented her from losing him.

She wasn't counting on keeping Lukas. She was going into this with her eyes open. It would be fine.

Still, when Lukas growled, "What are we waiting for?" into her ear, she felt a shiver of panic. But the feel of his lips on hers fed her desire, and she stopped fighting it and gave herself over to the need. She wrapped her arms around his neck and nuzzled his jaw.

Lukas lowered her to the bed, then settled next to her, a hand braced on either side of her. His eyes were dark, and yet she could see the hunger in them. And when he lowered his head and kissed her again, his mouth hot and hungry, Holly met his kiss with a hunger of her own.

Her hands slid over his back and the hard muscles of his arms and shoulders. While he was lean, his muscles were most definitely those of a man who worked hard physically. She loved running her fingers over him and feeling the tremor of those hard muscles beneath her hands.

Lukas's own hands were doing explorations of their

own, sliding beneath the hem of her T-shirt, tracing the line of the waistband of her shorts. Holly remembered how it felt to have his hands on her. He made her quiver. He made her moan.

The sound seemed to please him. Abruptly, Lukas shoved himself to his knees and drew her up with him to grab her shirt and pull it straight over her head. Then he sat back against his heels, a smile curving the corner of his mouth as he cupped her breasts in his palms.

Self-conscious despite her best intentions, Holly shifted to cover herself. But Lukas stilled her hands. "Don't."

His gaze settled on her, then he bent his head and kissed each of her breasts, teasing her nipples to hard, tight buds, made her gasp and grab his shoulders as his tongue skimmed over her heated flesh, leaving exquisitely sensitive trails.

Stardust trails, Holly thought, giving herself over to the moment—to the man.

And then she ceased to think at all.

Holly. In his bed.

At last.

Holly's hands on his bare back, nails scratching lightly, sent exquisite little bolts of electricity straight through him, making him even harder than he'd been. But when her fingers slid around to the snap at the waistband of his jeans, he stilled them even though his own fingers shook as he pulled hers away. "Wait." His breath came in quick gasps. He shoved himself back and up on one elbow.

Holly stared at him, eyes wide and uncomprehending. "Wait?"

"Just. Slow. Down." He could only manage one word at a time, and there was a tremor in his voice as well as in his hands. He felt like a teenager, lacking control, desperate for release. A release he craved at the same time he wanted this to last.

"No...hurry." His mouth twisted. "We've got...all night."

Then he dipped his head and buried his face in her hair, drawing in more deeply the tantalizing citrus scent that had always said "Holly" to him. He nibbled her ear, pressed kisses along her jaw, slid his hands down her sides, then up over her breasts.

"How come you get to do things?" Holly's voice was plaintive. He could hear a tremor in it that made him smile.

"Because you want me to." He lifted his head and looked down at her. "Don't you?"

She swallowed. It was answer enough. Still watching her face, he drew one trembling finger down between her breasts, circled her nipples, then bent his head to lave them again with his tongue. He smiled when he heard her breath catch.

"Lukas!" His name hissed between her teeth. She reached out and caught his hand in hers. But she didn't stop him. His lips pressed kisses where his fingers had gone. His tongue traced the same path, pebbling her nipples, making her squirm.

She trembled as he rubbed a thumb over the exquisite softness of her breasts, then cupped them, nuzzled and nibbled them. Holly let go of his hand to grab a handful of his hair. It made him smile, and he bent his head and moved lower, down across her flat belly to the waistband of her shorts. Then, as her hands slipped down to clutch his shoulders, he drew a fingertip along the edge of her waistband and felt the muscles in her abdomen contract. She shifted under his touch.

Lukas flicked open the button, then eased down the

zip and tugged the shorts down over her hips, then drew them down the length of her legs. Ah, those legs. God, he loved her legs.

Tossing the shorts aside, he made himself slow down, appreciate every moment as his fingers played back up from her ankles again. He followed them with his lips, kissing her knees, then sliding between them so he could do the same to the insides of her thighs.

"My turn," she said fiercely, pushing herself up to fumble with the zip of his jeans. He didn't stop her this time, even though he was on the edge and very nearly tipped right over when her fingers opened his zip and found him. Lukas's teeth clenched as her hand wrapped his hot flesh, tentatively at first, then more firmly. A harsh breath slipped between his teeth.

"Slow," he warned, teeth clenched.

It was close to the best thing he'd ever experienced— Holly touching him, learning his body—almost as wonderful as touching and learning hers. She could have shattered him right then if he'd let her. He wouldn't.

He stilled her fingers, then drew her hand away from him, felt the aching loss of her touch, but focused instead on her. He stroked lightly along the edge of the waistband of her panties, dipping beneath to trail a finger through the soft curls at the apex of her thighs. She trembled and shifted as he bent his head to plant a kiss there. And then another and another, before hooking his fingers around the scrap of lace and sliding them slowly down her thighs. Then he sat back and beheld Holly Montgomery Halloran naked before him.

"Dear God, you're beautiful."

He'd imagined this for years. Holly had figured so regularly in his nighttime fantasies, especially after the night of her prom, that he'd told himself that the real woman couldn't possibly live up to them.

But she did.

She was everything he had imagined—and more.

The curve of her hip, the length of her legs, the small pert mounds of her breasts, the triangle of curls that hid her mysteries all enticed him. He wanted to explore them all. First the soft smoothness of her skin drew his touch. He ran a hand over her from her shoulder over her hip, down her leg to her toes. He bent her leg, ignored the tantalizing hint of mystery that bending her knee uncovered, and instead kissed her toes.

"Lukas!"

"Mmm." He kissed them one by one, then let his fingers walk up her instep, trace her right ankle, then her left. Then he walked his fingers up her calves again to trace the backs of her knees, the exquisite softness of the insides of her thighs—torturing himself with anticipation. *Wait*, he told himself. *Wait*.

His thumbs brushed lightly against the curls where her thighs joined. Holly bit her lip, held perfectly still. She'd held still the night on his father's boat, too. She'd gripped his shoulders so hard she'd left tiny bruises that he'd cherished long after they had disappeared. And she'd let him touch her. He touched her now. More deeply. Slid a finger through folds that were wet. For him.

"Lukas!" Holly's voice was urgent.

"Mmm?" He breathed on her there.

"There is slow and then there is slow!" She sounded somewhere between lust and laughter.

Lukas laughed raggedly, then kissed her, touched his tongue to her. There.

She jerked. Her knees pressed against his ears. "You are driving me insane!"

"I know." He was driving himself insane, too.

"How would you like it if I did that to you?"

He groaned. "Do you think I'd tell you to stop?"

"Excellent." Abruptly Holly sat up and looped her fingers over the waistband of his jeans.

Lukas started to do it himself, but she batted his hands away. "My turn."

"Hol'—"

"We're going slow," she reminded him, all seriousness, then slanted him a wicked smile. "You'll love it."

She was going to kill him. He made a noise deep in his throat. But he knelt back on his heels stoically, watching as Holly came up on her knees before him in all her naked glory and slowly—inch by inch—no, centimeter by centimeter, slid the jeans down his hips, then coaxed him up off his heels to pull them off, to run her hands over him, taking her own sweet time.

He groaned, then gritted his teeth as she found him again and clasped him in both her hands, stroked him. His hips bucked. "Holly!"

She smiled. "Exactly."

Then she put a hand against his chest and pushed him back against the mattress. He reached for her, to pull her down on top of him. But she twisted away, moved to the end of the bed, bent her head, kissed his toes.

Lukas's fingers knotted around the sheet. "For God's sake!"

"See what I mean?" Holly looked up brightly with another of those maddening smiles. She slid between his legs, and he reached for her to lift her and settle her against him where he needed her most. If he didn't get her there soon—like, in an instant—it would be too late. Her merest touch would send him right over the edge. If she reached out a finger and touched him now, it would be all over.

"Wait, I thought you said—" Holly began, grinning at him.

But Lukas wasn't waiting any longer. "Enough waiting." He pulled her close, then rolled her back onto the bed and pressed his body against hers. He couldn't hold back, couldn't pace himself. Not now.

Holly didn't resist. She wrapped her arms and legs around him and opened to his kiss, to his need. She met him kiss for kiss, move for move, fitting her body, tight and hot and slick, to his, welcoming him in.

It was heaven. The years, the days, the minutes of tortured anticipation were over and even though Lukas did his best to make it last, he couldn't fight his need any longer. He slid into her, a single hard thrust, and she met him, digging her fingernails into his back as she arched against him. They shattered together.

And, as Lukas had known it would be, it was good.

The morning after.

Holly woke thinking those very words, and trying to articulate what had happened so she could put it in a box she would call My Affair with Lukas and then, in slightly less than six weeks' time, could close firmly and stick on a shelf at the back of her mind.

But at the moment, she just lay there in the early-morning light and watched Lukas sleep.

Lukas.

She had gone to bed with Lukas Antonides. Had had sex with Lukas Antonides. She had spent so many years

furious with him, or fighting with him or pretending he
didn't exist that it fairly boggled her mind.

She lay there, studying him, trying to think things
through, then deliberately stopped herself. There was
nothing to think about. She had no expectations. For six
weeks she was going to live in the moment. She wouldn't
let herself want anything else—wouldn't even let herself
consider anything else.

Just live, she told herself. *Be in the moment.* The moment, after all, was the only thing you ever really had.

And this was a moment she hadn't expected to ever
have—a time to contemplate Lukas unmoving except for
the soft draw and exhalation of his breath. That was novel
in itself. But so was seeing him looking young and unguarded.

Young, well, she had seen that before. But she didn't
think she had ever seen Lukas unguarded. The edgy
watchfulness or quicksilver enthusiasm she normally as-
sociated with his expressions were entirely absent. There
was a gentleness to his mouth now. His lips looked softer.
And heaven help her, Holly knew now exactly how soft
that was.

And how persuasive.

She wanted to curl up next to him and go back to sleep.
But she felt oddly energized, as well. And if she were
going to really be his gallery manager, she had unpacking
to do and material to read from the artists that Charlotte
had given her last night.

Besides, she didn't know what it would be like when
Lukas woke up. It could be awkward. Holly had no experience of "mornings after"—except with Matt. She didn't
know the protocol of brief affairs.

She slid out of bed and let herself take one last look
at him. She had six weeks with this man—as long as he

didn't tire of her sooner. But she wouldn't think about that, either. *Live for the moment*, she told herself again.

She would. For six weeks she would.

And then she would walk away unscathed.

When he awoke, Lukas was alone.

It was nearly nine. He hadn't slept till nine in years. But he'd slept like the dead after making love to Holly. He lay back and folded his arms under his head and grinned, energized, replete—and hungry all over again. He went downstairs and banged on the door to the gallery manager's apartment.

Holly opened it, color touching her cheeks as she looked up at him. "Hey." Her voice was soft, a little hesitant.

"Hey, yourself." And he hauled her into his arms and kissed her. She tasted like sunshine and apples and something singularly Holly. God, it was good. "Have you had breakfast?"

"Just this." She waved a half-eaten apple at him. "I'm still looking for my granola."

"We can find it later. I know a great brunch place." He grabbed her hand. "Come on."

"I should work." She gestured at the artists' info spread out on the bar.

But Lukas shook his head. "I'm your boss. I say we have brunch."

He took her to a little place not far from the gallery. It was unpretentious and undiscovered by any but the locals. But there were enough locals that they had to wait for a table.

Since he'd been back in the city, Lukas had found himself edgy, aware of too many people going too many places, always in a rush. Over all the years he'd been gone, he had grown used to space, to horizons, to the only noises being the ones he or those he was with made themselves. The cacophony that was New York had irritated him in a way he hadn't expected. And he hadn't been able to blot it out until now.

Being with Holly made the rest of the world recede. He wasn't busy thinking ahead, wondering where he needed to be next or what he needed to do.

He knew instinctively that he was right where he was supposed to be, sitting across a tiny table from the one woman who could make him laugh and think and want to argue, all within the space of a minute.

He might—oh, once or twice—have thought it would be nice to be back in bed with her. But it would happen, he promised himself.

"What are you smiling about?" Holly asked.

She had been telling him about Althea's upcoming wedding, and Lukas supposed he should be sympathetic. But it sounded like another of several weddings too many.

"Just thinking about taking you to bed," Lukas replied.

The color rose in her cheeks. She rolled her eyes. "Well, stop!"

"I like thinking about it. I like doing it. I thought you did, too." He raised a brow at her.

She focused on cutting her French toast. "Yes," she said.

Lukas grinned. "Good. Right, then. Althea's wedding. When is it?"

"End of July. Right before I leave." She told him the date.

"Same day as the reception," he said. "For the grant winners. It's going to be a big deal at the Plaza. The mayor and all that." He grimaced.

"Well, you probably won't have to wear pastel," Holly told him philosophically.

Lukas blanched. "Pastel?"

Holly smiled. "Never mind."

"Want a bite of my omelet?" He held out his fork to her.

She nibbled off it, then licked her lips. "Very tasty."

Lukas groaned. "Now can we talk about going back to bed?"

"No. We need to go back to the gallery so you can get me up to speed on this new job I've agreed to do."

So after one last cup of coffee, they headed back to the gallery where Lukas spent the rest of the afternoon on the gallery floor and then in the manager's office showing Holly the ropes, and periodically suggesting they go back upstairs as he had plenty of things he could show her there.

Holly just smiled and shook her head. She took her new job seriously, it seemed, peppering him with questions, half of which he didn't know the answers to. But he gave her the basics, explained the books, and gave her information about the opening coming up, and realized he should not have been so confident as to leave it all in Jenn's hands.

"She put some of it in place from Sydney." He knew that much. He said so as they walked back to her condo late that afternoon. They'd spent hours that could have been more interestingly occupied getting up to speed on work. "You can call her. You should call her. And I'll help as much as I can." He felt guilty handing the mess off to her. It had been a spur-of-the-moment suggestion, and he'd been amazed she had agreed. "Sera can help, too."

"It'll be a challenge." Holly unlocked her door and opened it. "But I'll do my best."

"Of course you will. And it'll be fine." He started to follow her in, but she turned to face him instead.

"So let me get going on it."

"What?"

"Go away. I have work to do."

"It's Sunday!" he protested.

"Which means I have one day to get my head around everything. I repeat, go away."

"But—"

"And don't pull out the 'I'm your boss' card," Holly said unrepentantly. "It's what you wanted—a trade-off, remember? I work for you, I get the apartment until I leave. We agreed," she reminded him. "And I mean what I say. I do what I say."

Holly kept her promises. She always had. It was why she'd been so angry with him the night of her prom: because she was engaged, she had made a promise to Matt and felt she had broken it with him. He raked a hand through his hair. "Fine. Go for it. If you have questions, follow the noise. I'm going to go find a wall to knock down."

She spent the rest of Sunday afternoon going over the artists' material, getting a feel for what they did, and then went back downstairs to see how it was displayed. She carried a notebook and made copious notes. And all the while she did so, she was aware of the sounds of destruction coming from upstairs. Lukas at work.

The thought made her smile. She could imagine him shirtless, working with a crowbar, muscles flexing and bunching. She wondered if he was wearing a tool belt. She was almost tempted to go up and see. But she didn't.

She was living in the moment—and the moment was here in the gallery, getting a grip on what she needed to do.

There would be time for Lukas later, she was sure of it.

And she was right. He banged on her door at seven

and said, "Enough work," in an authoritative tone. "Come and eat."

"I have to change. Where are we going?"

"To my place," he said. "And as far as I'm concerned, you don't have to wear anything at all."

She took a shower and put on clean clothes and went upstairs, reining in her skepticism about Lukas's ability to cook. But he really had made dinner—spaghetti and meat sauce, a fresh green salad and crusty hot garlic bread.

She was amazed. Matt couldn't boil water. She'd given up trying to teach him how to do anything in the kitchen. It was easier to do it herself. But it was wonderful to actually have a man cook for her—even one who had her out of her clothes and back in his bed before she could offer to wash the dishes.

"That's what dishwashers are for." Lukas was busy yanking his own clothes off, his gaze devouring her nakedness.

"Yes, but you have to load them," Holly protested.

"Not now. We have better things to do."

They did. They made love until the wee hours of the morning. Then they slept, wrapped in each other's arms.

Living in the moment, Holly thought, could be addictive.

She would have liked to spend all day there. But Lukas was already up and shaved. He was fixing breakfast when she emerged from the bedroom, still tender in places she had almost forgotten about.

"Morning." He kissed her with lingering thoroughness, then said, "Gotta stop that or I won't be meeting the mayor this morning." He set a bowl of oatmeal and raspberries in front of her.

"You're meeting the mayor?" Holly raised her brows.

"More likely one of his flunkies. We're going over lo-

gistics for the reception at the Plaza." He shot back his
cuff and consulted his watch. "And I'm going to be late.
Will you be okay here?"

"Of course," Holly said. "I've got my work cut out for
me."

"You don't have to," Lukas said.

"Oh? You got me here under false pretenses, did you?"
A corner of her mouth twitched.

"Any way I could get you," Lukas said. He snagged a
suit coat off the back of a chair and shrugged it on. "I'll
be back by lunchtime."

Holly finished her breakfast, then loaded the dishwasher with last night's dishes and this morning's, then
turned it on. She went back into Lukas's bedroom and
straightened the bed, letting herself remember how they'd
spent the night. Her cheeks grew warm just thinking about
it.

"Live in the moment," she reminded herself. Lukas
was heading uptown. It was time for her to get cleaned
up and go to work.

She turned up in Sera's office half an hour later to ask
for whatever material she had that she'd been saving for
Jenn. "Lukas said I should get it from you," she told his
assistant.

"You're the new gallery manager?" Sera's eyes were
like saucers. A knowing smile lit her face.

Holly felt her own cheeks reddening. "Just for six
weeks," she said. "Less if Lukas finds someone else."

"What happens in six weeks?"

So while Sera pulled up files and printed out material,
Holly told her about the Peace Corps.

Sera's surprise was evident. "You're going away? For
two years? And Lukas is okay with that?" she said doubtfully.

"It's not Lukas's decision," Holly told her.

"I wonder if he knows that," Sera murmured as she collated the material and put it in a folder.

Holly was sure Lukas knew it. She was sure it was exactly what he wanted. But she didn't say any of that to Sera. She just thanked her for the files and said she'd be back to pick her brain later.

The job, she discovered, was just as Lukas had said, not unlike teaching. The better you knew your students, the better job you could do. The same thing applied to the gallery. The more she knew about the artists and their work, the better job she could do promoting them with the public, and the more she could help them get the best out of the gallery and vice versa.

It was no hardship to get to know them better. They had stopped whatever they'd been doing on Saturday night to help her. She wanted to return the favor.

So besides going over the material Sera gave her, she went from studio to studio talking to the artists. She learned a lot about them, which she had expected. She also learned a good deal about Lukas, not just from what they told her, but from those blowup photos she hadn't had time to really look at the afternoon he'd first given her a tour.

They were photos of what she inferred were some of the mining sites where Lukas worked. They were blowups, of dirt and rubble and two dusty men, one much older, thin and wiry with gray hair buzzed close to his skull and wire-rimmed glasses perched on the end on his nose, the other lean, yet muscular, the ends of his normally sun-tipped locks even blonder in the harsh Australian sun.

They were candid shots, taken by friends, Holly presumed. But they captured well the relationship of Lukas and the old man. They were working together, talking together, standing together, covered with dust, their arms slung around each other's shoulders as they beamed at the camera. In the last shot they toasted each other with broad grins and pints of beer. Lukas looked as happy—and as satisfied—as she had ever seen him. And the pride in the old man's eyes was evident.

She understood very well why Lukas felt an obligation to see Skeet's foundation was a success. The rapport between them was obvious. It was beautiful.

It gave her a greater appreciation for Lukas than she'd had before. She'd known him as a boy and as a self-absorbed young man. She didn't see that here. She saw something deeper, something valuable.

What she saw there, she soon discovered, extended to the attitude of the artists toward the man who owned the gallery.

"He understands us," Charlotte told her.

"He listens," Teresa said. And she went on to tell Holly about how it was when she'd whined to him about lack of opportunities, that he'd said, "What would make it better?"

"I just babbled," Teresa told her. "Told him how wonderful it would be to have access to a North American market, to be promoted on the other side of the world. I didn't see it ever happening. I was just talking. But he made it happen."

"He lets us alone," Charlotte said. "He doesn't try to get us to do particular things. He never makes suggestions. Not even about how we display our work in his gallery. He's determined that it's ours, not his."

Not one person said, *He's bossy. He's autocratic. He thinks he knows it all.*

He certainly wasn't micromanaging her. He found her when he came back at lunchtime and asked if she wanted peanut butter and jelly or pâté de foie gras.

"What?" Holly was behind the desk in the main gallery reading over a spreadsheet.

He repeated it. "I've got peanut butter upstairs. Or I can take you out."

"I need to keep going. Jenn left a list of appropriate region-specific foods, but I have to find a caterer who can actually make them." It was a good idea to serve Australian, New Zealand and Pacific finger foods and desserts. But it was going to take a bit of effort to come up with a provider.

"Fine, but you have to eat," Lukas said, drawing her to her feet.

"I need to make phone calls."

"Right. Peanut butter and jelly it is."

He made a mean peanut butter and jelly sandwich. Holly had to give him that. But after he did he let her go back to work. He didn't turn up every ten minutes to make suggestions or to boss her around. There was the normal amount of noise in the gallery until about four o'clock, when the pre-opening hours closed to the public.

Then the banging and hammering began. Holly found she actually liked hearing it. She liked the images it called to mind. But when it stopped just after six, she found that her imagination was lacking.

Moments after it ended, Holly looked up to catch her breath at the sight of a sweaty, grimy, shirtless Lukas Antonides standing in her office doorway, wearing jeans— and a tool belt. Holly swallowed at the sight.

"Time to quit," he said.

"No more walls to knock down?"

"Not if I want the building to keep standing. Let's take a shower."

"Lukas!"

He grinned unrepentantly. "Come on, Hol'. You know you want to wash my back."

She wanted to wash a great deal more than that. She wanted to wash all of him. Holly swallowed a whimper. Then she drew an anticipatory breath and stood up. "All right. Let's."

Sometimes over the days that followed, Lukas felt as if he'd died and gone to heaven.

He had Holly in the office, bright-eyed and eager, yet still businesslike, every day. He had Holly in the kitchen—sometimes his and sometimes hers—for breakfasts and dinners. She was a good cook—and she ate his own attempts with relish.

"A man to cook for me?" she said. "Be still my beating heart."

His own heart beat a whole lot more rapidly when she was around. He had expected that the reality of Holly might well pale compared to his youthful dreams of her. How often, after all, did the real thing ever measure up?

But Holly more than measured up. The memories of her had always outshone any girl or woman Lukas had ever dated. But she outdid herself, as well.

For a man who had always had his eye on the horizon, who'd spent his life in pursuit of what was beyond it, this was a whole new experience.

He didn't want it to end. What the hell did Holly need to go halfway around the world to find herself for? She was doing fine right here with him.

There was no question that taking Holly to bed was amazing. But they got along well outside of bed, too. He remembered she used to like baseball so he'd invited her along to his softball games. She came and cheered him on.

He tried to get her to come with him to the boatyard

where he worked on Wednesday afternoons and Saturday mornings with the St. Brendan's kids. "You want to come," he said because she quizzed him eagerly about everything when he came back.

But she wouldn't come. She told him, "I have work to do."

"Work can wait," he told her.

But she shook her head. "It's my job." And Holly was determined to do what she had promised to do.

He had no complaints. The minute she'd taken over as gallery manager, things started getting done. She didn't know everything that needed doing. She wasn't familiar with galleries and artists and who the people to know were. But she figured out very quickly who to ask. She even called Grace and asked her advice.

"Grace Marchand?" Lukas stared at her, surprised. She was making dinner in his kitchen, looking completely at home. He liked coming in at night to find her there. "You know Grace?"

"No, but you do." Holly tore up lettuce for a salad with brisk efficiency. "I said I was working for you, and I needed some advice. She was happy to help. We're having lunch together tomorrow. You're not invited," she informed him cheerfully.

And thank God for that, Lukas thought. But he couldn't help wondering how things were going the next afternoon. And he made it a point to turn up in her office to remind her about his softball game that afternoon.

"How was Grace?" he asked, just a little warily.

"She's brilliant. She'd make a great gallery manager," Holly told him. "All the right connections. She can get anything in the city done before dinner. Seriously, Lukas, you might think about it. I can see why your mother thinks you ought to marry her."

"No," Lukas said firmly. "Just no," he said again when her eyes widened at his vehemence. "Not interested."

Holly let out a sigh. "Well, you'd better find someone," she said. "It's not that long until I leave."

She still talked about leaving. There was a copy of her itinerary tacked to the bulletin board in her office—and some Peace Corps official mail reminding what inoculations she was expected to have before she left.

"Good thing I'm not needle-phobic," she said cheerfully the day she went to get her typhoid shot.

Lukas found he wished she were. And he didn't like being asked his opinion about what sort of clothing she should plan on taking to a South Pacific climate.

It was all he could do not to tell her to forget the South Pacific climate, that she was staying right here. But if he told her that, then what? He kept his mouth shut.

In bed they didn't have to talk about inoculations or proper attire or anything else. They made love. And there, too, Holly exceeded expectations. She was as willing, eager and inventive a lover as he could have hoped for. And she welcomed his lovemaking with passion and enthusiasm.

He daydreamed his way through the grant applications, doing his best to whittle them down. His heart caught in his throat when he watched her at work, nibbling on the end of her pen as she contemplated something she was reading, or licking her lips at the sight of a particularly tasty snack one of the artists brought in, and his mind flashed back to those lips on him, that tongue making him crazy with need.

He was going crazy right now. He'd just come back from a meeting at the Plaza and stopped by her office to discover her at her desk, sucking her pen as she read.

Holly looked up. "Oh. You're back." She smiled. "Did

you say something?" She twirled the pen across her lips again, then ran her tongue over the top of it.

Lukas felt blood pumping where it had no business pumping at the office in the middle of the day. He started to straighten, then changed his mind and cleared his throat instead. "No. And stop teasing."

"Me?" Holly looked briefly surprised, then gave him a smug grin. "Hadn't realized I was." But the speculative look in her eyes made his temperature go up another notch.

"You realized." And if she hadn't at first, she certainly did now. "You want me to make love to you right here in the office?"

Holly tipped her head, a smile playing at her lips. "Is that a threat?" she asked. "Or a promise?"

Holly had never thought of herself as wanton. She never would have considered making love with Matt on a desk in the middle of the afternoon. But Lukas brought out the devil in her, the one who, when pushed, had learned how to push back, the one who was determined to grab these few weeks and live them to the fullest.

And why not? They were two consenting adults. They knew each other well—well enough to press each other's buttons, especially now that Matt was no longer there to be the steadying influence between them.

If Lukas could stand there, leaning against the doorjamb of her office looking sexy as sin in a light tan suit, a dark brown shirt and a green, jungle-patterned tie that brought out the gold in his hair and the jade in his eyes, why shouldn't she flirt a little in return?

"If you keep looking at me like that, it's a promise." Lukas shoved away from the doorjamb, pushed the door shut and locked it behind him.

Holly felt a kick of desire go straight through her as he advanced purposefully across the room. She stood and came around the desk, meeting him head-on. "How nice you had a meeting with the mayor," she said, purring as she reached for him—and his tie. She loosened it and slipped it off his neck. "I think I can find a use for this."

She found a use for it. Several. Both on the sofa in his office and later that night in his bed.

It was heady and exhilarating, making love with Lukas. He brought out a side of her she'd never known she had. With Matt things had been steady, calm and responsible—even their lovemaking. With Lukas, it went from fiery to tender, from passionate to gentle. With Lukas, anything went.

An affair with Lukas was everything she'd ever imagined it would be. And more.

Sated from their loving, she curled against his side, feeling her heart rate begin to slow. But her desire didn't slow. She raised her head and looked at him, traced his features, memorized them.

She wanted… No, she didn't.

She wouldn't let herself want. But sometimes she caught herself wishing… And she knew she couldn't even let herself wish.

Because he was Lukas. He was the man with his gaze on the horizon. He made no long-term commitments. He traveled light.

And even if he stayed in New York, he would move on from her. So she needed to move first.

"Remember that," Holly murmured, and she settled once more into the curve of Lukas's shoulder and laid a hand against his chest.

Lukas lifted his head and turned it to look at her. "Remember what?" His voice sounded soft and smoky across her cheek.

Holly hesitated, then tamped down the desire for more and shifted to press a kiss to his whisker-roughened jaw. Then she let her hand slide slowly down his chest, across his taut belly, then lower. She would take her joy where she found it. Here. Now.

She wouldn't ask for more.

CHAPTER NINE

THE GALLERY OPENING was a resounding success. All because of Holly.

Lukas was delighted and justified. He'd hired her, after all.

Holly, of course, credited everyone else. Lukas knew better. She might have got the names of useful people and lists of things that needed to be done from other more knowledgeable people, but Holly had done them. She had made it happen.

And she was the one who moved effortlessly among the guests now, smiling and talking with them, extolling the virtues of this artist and the vision of that one.

She had taken the time to get to know each one of them, both as artists and as people. As he watched her introduce Charlotte to the mayor, Lukas grinned. Normally painfully shy, Charlotte had blossomed under Holly's nurturing support.

"She's fantastic," his sister-in-law, Tallie, murmured into Lukas's ear as she followed his gaze. "A good choice, Lukas," she added with a smile.

"Yep." Lukas leaned against the wall, knowing he should be out there, too, glad-handing the visitors, schmoozing with journalists and hobnobbing with the bigwigs. But for just a moment he took a step back, let himself watch, let himself dream.

It wasn't too far-fetched to imagine doing this with Holly again. Doing this with Holly forever.

Forever? As in…what? Ask her to marry him?

He waited for the notion to feel like a punch in the gut. The idea of getting married had always felt like that before.

When Tallie had mentioned marrying Grace, the very thought had him envisioning a life sentence, a noose around his neck. Grace was a great person. Terrific girl. Smart. Capable. Beautiful. Not one he could ever imagine spending a lifetime with. Nor was any girl he'd ever dated. Marriage in the abstract he believed in. Antonides men married.

Except sometime in the past couple of years he'd begun wondering if he wasn't the exception who proved the rule. He'd reached the age of thirty-two and he hadn't had the least inclination to propose to spend his life with anyone.

He watched as Holly, having got the mayor and Charlotte talking, turned away, already looking around to see what else needed doing. Her gaze traveled the room, lit on him, and when their gazes connected, she smiled.

No, in his entire life, Lukas hadn't ever wanted to propose to anyone.

Until now.

In December, when she'd agreed to a two-year stint in the Peace Corps, Holly had begun counting the days until her training began. And she'd marked them off with increasing enthusiasm as time passed.

Two weeks ago she had stopped counting.

She wasn't even aware she had done so until the

Wednesday after the gallery opening. Lukas had left the bed before dawn, going to meet Elias and sail a boat with him out to Greenport for one of Elias's customers.

It was one of the rare mornings since she'd moved here that she'd awakened alone, without Lukas's arms around her or her burrowed into his side. Refusing to lie there and focus on the awareness of how much she missed him, Holly jumped out of bed and went to shower.

It was while she was making herself a bowl of cereal that she noticed her calendar and realized for the first time that several days weren't marked off. More than several. Two and a half weeks' worth of days. The last day she'd marked off was the day she had moved out of her condo.

The day she and Lukas had begun their affair.

Affair. It meant temporary. Shallow. Meaningless. Nothing more than an itch to be scratched. Obviously the attraction wasn't going away by ignoring it. She'd tried that. *So do something about it*, she'd told herself. *Have a fling. Discover that Lukas Antonides is everything you ever thought he was—gorgeous, sexy, talented, energetic— but also impetuous, inconstant, egotistical.*

She had been sure she would be ready to walk away when the time came. She'd imagined she'd be ready to run!

But she wasn't even crossing off the days on the calendar. She was living in the moment—and enjoying every minute of it. But the fear was growing inside her that she had made a mistake, that she'd tempted fate by going to bed with Lukas.

That she was falling in love with him.

No! No, she wasn't. She couldn't be. She wouldn't let herself!

It was just that she was alone, that Lukas wasn't there

to distract her. "Might not be back until Thursday," he'd told her last night, grimacing as he relayed the news. "Depends on how much time Elias has to spend getting the buyer up to speed. And if he wants to stop and see the folks on the way home."

Lukas's parents still lived on the shore in the big house where he had grown up. Holly knew from things he had said over the past couple of weeks that, for all that he'd been away a dozen years, Lukas was close to his family.

"You should stop and see them," Holly said.

"I would," he said, "if you came along. You could stop and see your mother."

"And tell her I'm living with you?" Holly hadn't even told her mother she'd sold the condo yet. She hadn't wanted to explain why she'd moved to Lukas's. She knew what her mother would think—that she was foolish, she'd get hurt, she should never take such a risk—and she didn't want to hear it.

"You're not living with me," Lukas pointed out. "You have your place. I have mine."

"But we seem to be in the same place a great deal of the time," she reminded him, nuzzling his whiskered cheek. "But we don't need to be together every minute. I have work to do here. A job, remember?"

"I never got to take you sailing."

"Another time."

"Promise?"

"Yes. Of course. As long as we do it before the first of August. Enjoy the day with Elias. Go see your parents. Don't even think about me."

But she thought about him.

It was because the opening was over and she had time to breathe, she told herself. It was because he wasn't there in front of her, coming up with ideas, making demands, distracting her, teasing her, kissing her. But all day long her mind was filled with a kaleidoscope of images.

She helped Teresa hang a new painting and remembered Lukas on a ladder, hanging another one, scowling as he tried to make sure it was perfectly straight. She fixed a peanut butter sandwich for lunch and smiled at her visions of Lukas slapping jam on bread as he made her lunch. Back down in her office, her mind went immediately to Lukas in black tie the night of the gallery opening, looking far handsomer than any man had a right to. She had another memory of him that night as well—of him bending down to listen to his grandmother lecture him. Then she had straightened his tie and patted his cheek as if he were a small boy. And Lukas had kissed her. The memory made Holly's eyes well.

He was so good with all his family. His grandmother, his parents, his siblings, even Martha, who was at pains to give him grief. He doted on his nephews and nieces. She had visions of Lukas with his nephews swarming around him, grinning broadly as he hoisted his niece onto his shoulders so she could be princess of them all.

She sat at her desk and tried to focus on writing a press release. But the last time she'd tried, Lukas had carried her off to bed. And of course, then she couldn't help but close her eyes and see Lukas naked in her bed, eyes slumberous, yet hungry and intent, focusing just on her.

"Ah, there you are!"

Holly jumped a foot as Althea swooped into her office, all smiles, and with a dress carrier bag over her arm. "Look what I've got!"

Holly felt a sinking sensation. "Oh. How nice."

Althea rolled her eyes. "Oh, ye of little faith. You'll love it. Truly. Stig says it's you. I just hope you won't outshine the bride," Althea added wryly.

"No chance of that. You've always been a beautiful bride."

Althea laughed. "All that practice. But Stig picked my dress, too, so I'm feeling pretty confident." She thrust the dress bag at Holly. "I'm just the messenger, and I'm late for a hair appointment. Let me know how it fits. If you need alterations, we can get them done next week." And she was gone as quickly as she'd come.

The dress bag hung over the back of a chair in her office the rest of the afternoon. Holly ignored it, even though it began to take on the proportions of an elephant in the room. She carried it upstairs after work, but she didn't take it out of the bag. She didn't want to be depressed. Then Charlotte and Teresa and a sculptress called Gwen invited her to go out for pizza.

"Since Lukas is gone," Teresa said, "we thought you might come."

Holly went. And after the pizza, Charlotte headed back to work on a wall hanging, but the other two wanted to go clubbing.

"Come with us," Gwen urged her and Teresa nodded her head.

Holly couldn't remember the last time she'd gone clubbing. Maybe after she and Matt were first married. Another lifetime ago. It wasn't her scene. But if she went back to the apartment, she knew what would happen. She would be faced with the dress—and she would miss Lukas.

"I'll come," she said.

It was nearly midnight when they left the club, and just past when Holly let herself into the building and climbed the stairs to her apartment.

"Stay in mine," Lukas had suggested. "Then I could come home and find you in my bed."

Holly had shaken her head firmly. "I'm sleeping in my bed."

But faced with it—as big and white and empty as an Alaskan winter—she was tempted to go upstairs. There, of course, she would find an even bigger bed, but it would have Lukas's scent on the pillows. And she could sleep in the T-shirt he'd worn yesterday.

Which just went to show how far gone she was, Holly thought, disgusted with herself.

August had better hurry up and get there. She was getting too soppy for her own good. But at the same time, she didn't want it to come at all.

Her brain muddled, Holly took a shower. But there were reminders of Lukas there, too. Yesterday morning she'd washed his back, had trailed her fingers down its muscular planes, then had slid her hands around to soap the front of him. Her body heated again now remembering the feel of slick, firm flesh beneath her fingers, and remembering what had happened after.

Abruptly, she shut the water off and got out of the shower. It was when she was putting on sleep shorts and a T-shirt—her own—that she spied the carrier bag with the bridesmaid dress hanging on the closet door.

She wanted to ignore it. But if it needed alterations, she would have to get them done. Wearing a frilly cupcake dress was bad enough. Wearing one that didn't fit would be even worse.

She slid the zip down on the carrier bag and opened it, then stared. "Oh, my word."

Anything less like a cupcake would have been hard to imagine.

The dress was red, a deep, vivid red. A dark, sultry lipstick of a color. There wasn't a frill or a flounce or a furbelow in sight. There wasn't much material at all, to be honest. It was a minimalist sort of dress, Holly decided as she took it out of the bag and gave it a shake. She sucked in her breath.

Very minimal indeed. And elegant. And sexy. And Stig thought it was "her"?

She had never worn anything quite so clearly sexy in her life.

Heart beating faster now, Holly slipped it on, then twirled in front of the mirror, astonished at the picture she made. The dress fit perfectly, molding her curves smoothly without being tight. The nearly shoulder-to-shoulder neckline plunged in a vee to the tops of her breasts, accentuating the soft roundness hidden beneath the silk. Three-quarter-length sleeves hugged her arms, giving the dress a sophistication that bare arms would not. And the flare of the hem just above her knees swirled, making the silk rustle as Holly turned in front of the mirror.

"Can I rip that off you?"

Holly spun around to see Lukas standing in the doorway. She felt a kick somewhere in the region of her heart. "You came back? It's one o'clock in the morning!"

"Didn't want to miss curfew." He crossed the room. "Couldn't stay away from you," he said in a low, rough voice, reaching for her.

"Don't touch! Althea will kill me if anything happens to this dress."

"This is the cupcake?" Lukas looked astonished.

"It's not a cupcake," Holly admitted. "Be careful!" she cried as he spun her around and moved in to nuzzle her neck.

"Then don't wear enticing dresses." He kissed her nape, sending shivers down her spine. Holly squirmed. "Hold still," he muttered as he slid the zip down carefully, then skimmed the dress off her shoulders.

It dropped to the floor, leaving her naked to his gaze. Lukas's breath hissed between his teeth. "God almighty, Hol'!" His voice was strangled.

"I just got out of the shower," she said defensively. She scooped up the dress, holding it in front of her, as if he hadn't seen it all before. "Then I remembered I hadn't tried it on. Althea needed to know if it needed alterations."

"It doesn't need alterations." He still sounded stunned.

Holly felt wobbly at the sight of him. "I didn't think you were coming back tonight." She fumbled with the dress and the hanger.

"You're the one who's going to wreck it." Lukas took it out of her hands and hung it up again. "I came home because you're here. But you weren't in my bed."

"Because you weren't there."

Lukas took her in his arms. "No worries," he said and scooped her up in his arms, carrying her into her bedroom. "We've got a bed right here."

Every day Holly lived in the moment.

She said yes to going out to his parents' place in the Hamptons for the Fourth of July. She played with his nieces and nephews and chatted with his brothers and sisters and even smiled in the face of his grandmother's obvious approval, even though she knew Lukas's *yiayia* believed there was more going on between them than was really there.

It wasn't her job to protect Lukas's family from their misinterpretations, she told herself. Let him explain after she was gone. But even though she told herself that, she couldn't help feeling guilty.

"I don't like lying to your family," she told him after they were back in the city.

"Well, stay then," he said.

Holly looked at him, startled. Then she shook her head. "No, I can't."

She refused to let herself be tempted by the idea. He didn't mean it. He didn't love her. He didn't want to marry her. And even if he did…

Holly wouldn't even let her mind go there.

Live in the moment. It was her mantra. She said it a dozen times a day as the weeks went on. And she was having a wonderful time, she had to admit that.

They went kayaking one weekend. It was fun to camp out with Lukas. Very different from similar trips she'd taken with Matt. Lukas was more spontaneous and, surprisingly, more willing to listen to her suggestions. Lukas had seemed a little apprehensive about taking her when she'd wished aloud that she could go kayaking one more time before she left. But once they got there, he was fine. They even talked a bit about Matt, and it seemed to take the edge off his apprehension.

"I thought it might make you sad," he told her on the way home.

"I thought it might, too," Holly said honestly. "But I just had a good time. Thank you."

The next weekend they kept his nephews from Saturday afternoon until Sunday night. It had been Digger's idea. He and Holly had hit it off when he discovered that she knew the names of all kinds of road-grading equipment and had half a dozen kids' books about it.

"I'll give them to you," she promised Digger. "A few less things to keep in my storage area," she told Lukas.

"Can I have them now?" Digger asked, eyes bright.

"How about next Saturday?"

"Can we have a sleepover?" Digger wanted to know.

"Of course," Holly said.

"I only have sleepovers with you," Lukas complained that night.

"Not next Saturday," Holly told him. "You know you're glad to have them. And it will give Elias and Tallie a bit of a break."

"Nobody's giving me a break," Lukas muttered.

But they'd all had a good time. Digger had even looked at Holly and said, "We should keep her," to his uncle when the boys were going home.

"Suits me," Lukas said.

Holly told herself to not even think about it. But it was getting harder and harder to live for the moment when the moments seemed to want to add up to something more. Of course that was only in her mind, and Holly knew it.

She couldn't tell what was in Lukas's mind. Most of the time he was all smiles, charm and good conversations. But sometimes he grew remote, distracted. At night when they made love, he could be tender and gentle or passionate, almost desperately intense. Maybe he was tiring of her and didn't know how to say so. Maybe he was trying to recapture the enthusiasm of their first days together.

Holly didn't know. She didn't dare ask.

She just told herself it would be good when August finally got here. Soon their affair would be over. They would go their separate ways.

Holly knew Lukas couldn't go to Althea's wedding with her. It was the same day that the MacClintock grant recipients were being feted along with recipients of several other grants at the Plaza. Lukas had to be there.

So she was surprised when he came out of the bedroom, still knotting his tie, that morning and said, "Save me a dance."

"A dance?"

"At the reception." He was looking remote and distracted, though, even as he said it, and she wondered why he had.

"You won't have time to come to the reception."

He shot her a moody look as he shrugged into his suit coat. "I'll be there."

He wouldn't be.

Holly knew Lukas. Lukas dealt with what was in front of him. He was a man who responded to the moment, and today would be full of moments requiring him to deal with the MacClintock Foundation winners, the mayor and lots of other movers and shakers of the Big Apple. He wouldn't have a moment to think about her.

Which was, Holly assured herself, actually just as well.

They only had a few days left. She needed to wean herself away from Lukas, stop thinking about him day and night.

Althea's wedding was a perfect chance to do that. Just as Lukas wouldn't have time to think of her today, she'd barely have a moment to give him a thought. It was a relief to get to the hotel where the wedding party was changing into their finery. She was hustled up in one of the elevators to the thirtieth floor where Althea, her mother, a hairstylist and a makeup artist swooped down upon her.

"Hairstylist? Makeup artist?" Holly gave Althea a wide-eyed disbelieving look. None of her other weddings had required such expertise.

Althea shrugged. "I've got a famous groom. What can you do? There's press here. I don't want them to think Stig is marrying beneath himself."

"He's not," Holly assured her.

"But there will be stories," Althea's harried mother, Laura, said. "Stig and Althea haven't made it a secret that

Althea has had a bit of trouble, er, making up her mind. The least we can do is look elegant and put-together."

Elegant and put-together sounded like a plan. Holly did her best to get with the program, to focus on the wedding, all the while wondering where Althea found the courage to give her heart all over again. Sometimes Althea seemed shallow, vague and flighty. Today, though, Holly thought she was incredibly brave.

"Sit." The stylist pointed Holly to a chair. "We don't have much time."

This wedding was a bigger madhouse than any of Althea's other weddings had been, and yet Holly recognized that this time there was a sense of rightness that the others had lacked. Maybe it was the look Holly saw in Stig's eyes as he looked past her to watch Althea come toward him down the aisle. Maybe it was the tears that had brimmed in Althea's when she spoke her vows. Or the way they kissed the first time as man and wife.

Holly didn't know. But as the wedding turned into the reception, as Stig and Althea danced together, were toasted and celebrated, smashed wedding cake in each other's faces and never ever stopped smiling, she knew she was happy for them, happier than she'd been at any of Althea's other weddings.

She sat at the head table and watched them swirl around the floor once more, this time in the company of many of the other guests, and she smiled, too. Theirs was the way weddings should be. For once she didn't compare it to her own wedding. Barely even thought about it.

"Dance with me."

Startled, Holly turned and looked up.

Lukas stood behind her, a somber expression on his face.

"What's wrong?"

"Nothing's wrong." His tone was almost curt.

"But…the Plaza? The mayor—?"

"The mayor is charming the first MacClintock Foundation grant winners and their extended families. Probably enough people to win him the next election. He couldn't be happier. Dance with me," Lukas said again and held out his hand, waiting for her.

But even as he did the music ended. The next piece was moody, almost plaintive, with lots of soulful clarinets. It touched a chord deep in Holly's breast. Echoed the way she felt.

One last dance. One more memory. Savor it, she told herself, and she put her hand in his and stood.

Effortlessly, Lukas steered her onto the dance floor and took her in his arms. It felt warm and right. The place she ought to be. And Holly couldn't resist. She let herself be wrapped in his embrace.

More than let. Relished it, drew strength from it, sustenance. So much for weaning herself away. She laid her cheek against the smooth summer wool of his jacket, felt the easy glide of muscle beneath, and gave herself over to the music, to the moment.

To the man.

When it ended, Lukas said, "Let's get out of here."

"I'm the bridesmaid!"

"They're married," Lukas said impatiently. "Your job is done."

And once more he drew her with him, this time toward Althea and Stig, who were in conversation with Althea's parents. *Matt's* parents.

"Say goodbye," Lukas instructed her.

But before Holly could open her mouth, Matt's dad, Joe, stuck out his hand to greet Lukas. Then Laura wrapped him in a warm embrace. "We've missed you," she murmured. "So glad you're back. You must come out and see us."

"I will," Lukas promised, the huskiness in his voice telling Holly that his promise was more than perfunctory. "Soon. We have to leave now."

All four—Stig and Althea, Joe and Laura—turned their gazes from Lukas to Holly. Four sets of eyebrows lifted. Althea was, of course, the first to speak.

"Of course you do!" she said with every bit of warmth of which Althea was capable—which Holly knew from years of experience was a lot.

"I don't have to," Holly began. "If you need me to stay…"

"I think I am the one she'll be needing now." Stig gave her a grin and a wink. "Nice dress, don't you think?" he said to Lukas.

"Very nice." Lukas's voice was clipped, his arm possessive around her. *I can hardly wait to get her out of it.* Holly heard the words as if he'd spoken them aloud. She was sure Stig did, too.

"Go," Althea said, making shooing motions. "I'll call you when we get back from our honeymoon."

Holly nodded. She wouldn't be here, but Althea was a smart woman. She'd figure it out.

Lukas had brought his Porsche. He tucked her into it wordlessly, then went around and got in the driver's side. If Holly had thought the cab of his truck shrank when he got in, it was nothing compared to the suddenly minuscule confines of the Porsche. She looked over at him, willing him to smile.

But he'd gone into one of his distracted moods. He put the car in gear and they were off.

Another night he would be regaling her with stories of the event with the mayor and the grant recipients, charming her, making her laugh as she saw it through his eyes. Lukas could do that. He'd done it millions of times. Notably, she recalled, the night of her senior prom.

But tonight he drove straight through Saturday-evening midtown traffic, jaw tight, eyes straight ahead.

Fingers knotted in her lap, Holly didn't speak, either. But by the time they reached Union Square, her nerves were beyond frayed. "What's wrong?"

"Nothing's wrong." But there was an edge to his voice.

"Tell me."

"Not now" His fingers flexed on the steering wheel. He stared straight ahead, focusing on heavy midtown traffic.

Holly turned in the seat to see him better. "Lukas, what's going on?"

"Just wait."

"Since when can't you drive and talk at the same time?"

His jaw bunched. "I can't drive and propose marriage at the same time!"

Holly stared at him, stunned. "What?"

"Oh, hell." He shot her a hard look. "You heard me."

Had she? Holly swallowed. Marriage? Lukas was proposing…marriage? She couldn't find any words.

"Would it be such a bad thing?" Lukas demanded. "I thought we had a good month." He hit her with the glare again. "Didn't you think we had a good month?"

"Yes," she said faintly. "But…"

"But what?"

"It was an…affair." Just saying it made it sound weak and insubstantial. Nothing like what she'd experienced. And yet…

"An affair?" Lukas fairly spat the words. "So, I was just an itch you wanted to scratch?"

"As I was for you," Holly retorted.

"You're more than an itch," Lukas told her. He slammed

on the brakes at a red light and cursed under his breath. "You couldn't wait, could you? You had to push."

"Me, push?" Holly gave a sharp laugh.

"You could have waited till we got home."

"You could have acted less like you were going to the dentist!"

They glared at each other. Holly looked away first.

"It's green," she said. "The signal."

Lukas ground his teeth and stomped on the gas pedal. Neither of them said another word until they reached the door of her apartment.

There, Holly fumbled with the key in nerveless fingers until Lukas took it away and opened the door for her. "Thank you," she said primly. "Good night."

But of course, Lukas came in before she could shut the door on him. "I love you, damn it," he said raggedly. "I want to marry you."

"'I love you, damn it'?" Holly echoed.

He raked a hand through his hair. "You know what I mean! It's more than an itch, Holly. It's a future. You feel it. You know you do." He reached out and caught her by the arm, hauling her against him. "You love me, too."

Holly didn't deny it. She didn't fight him. Couldn't. She wanted him too much.

She knew the depth of her foolishness, then. She had lied to herself when she'd believed she could have these few weeks with Lukas and walk away from him satisfied and unscathed. She had thought that being aware was being in control. She was wrong. It would hurt.

But staying would hurt worse. She had to go.

But not yet. Not without this—this touch of his lips, the warmth of his arms around her, the silkiness of his hair threaded through her fingers, his hands skimming down the zip on her sexy dress, then easing it off her shoulders, letting it slither to a pool at her feet.

"You love me," Lukas whispered against her ear. "And I love you."

Then he lifted her and carried her into the bedroom and laid her gently on the bed. His eyes were hooded, the skin taut across his cheekbones, his lips barely parted, breathing softly and close—so close she could feel the heat of his breath on her cheek.

She took his face between her hands and ran her thumbs across his brows, then across those sharply sculpted cheekbones, memorizing each detail before pressing her lips to his.

Lukas groaned. He toed off his shoes, then sat up, fumbling to drag off his tie and undo the buttons of his shirt.

Holly's hands wrapped his, held them still. "Let me. Please." Her throat ached as she spoke.

Lukas let out a harsh breath. "Go ahead then."

She took her time, slipped the tie off his neck, then with fingers almost as unsteady as his, she undid the buttons one by one, tugged his shirttails out of his trousers and pulled it off, then skimmed his undershirt over his head. Pressing kisses to his chest, she brought her hands down to his belt buckle, worked it open, slid a hand in to caress him.

"Hol'," he warned, his hips surging against her. She would have taken longer, would have had him as strung out as she had been that night so many years ago. But Lukas was done with that. His patience gone, he peeled off his trousers and shorts, shed his socks and bore her back onto the bed.

Then he had his way with her, took his time, kissed his way from her breastbone to the apex of her thighs. He settled between her legs and skimmed his fingers up them, then parted her, touched her, stroked her.

Holly tried to hold still, but couldn't. She twisted beneath the friction of his fingers as they heightened her pleasure. And then he moved over her, came down to her and entered her fully, and the two of them were one.

For an instant he held himself still, his gaze dark and intense bare inches above hers. "I love you, Holly. I've always loved you." The words were harsh and hoarse. They seemed dragged from the depths of his being. Holly's fists clutched the sheets, her toes curled as he began to move. Slowly. Deeply. As if he were touching the very core of her being.

If she let him, he could touch her there. She knew it. She nearly sobbed with the knowledge. She twisted, matching his thrusts, letting go of the sheet to rake her fingernails down his back, then clutching him close as he drove them both over the edge.

She cried out. She said his name.

He slumped against her, his body sweat-slick, his heart hammering so hard she could feel it against her own. He lifted his head and looked down at her, a hint of a smile on his lips. "So," he said raggedly, "you want to argue with that?"

Holly couldn't argue. She couldn't even speak. She just looked at him, drank him in. Then she shut her eyes and breathed deeply, held him close.

The sun was high in the sky when Lukas woke. He knew where he was, tangled in the sheets of Holly's bed. He remembered the passion, the intensity, the love they had shared. And he smiled, recalling how she'd simply shut her eyes and gone to sleep beneath him. He'd lain there, savoring the feel of her body, nearly boneless now, slumbering beneath him. Finally, he'd rolled off, but only to tuck her against his chest and spoon his legs behind hers.

He sighed with contentment, then stretched and rolled over to reach for her again.

He was alone.

CHAPTER TEN

SHE WAS IN the kitchen. Or in the bathroom. She'd gone to her office. Or maybe down to the gallery to work.

Lukas bolted out of bed, then told himself that the flare of panic he'd felt at finding her gone was nothing more than an overactive imagination.

She hadn't left him. She couldn't have.

But it turned out his imagination was better informed than all his rationalizations. He found a note on the kitchen counter. As he picked it up, his hand shook.

Lukas, thank you for everything. I won't see you again before I go. It's better this way. I'll have a mover pack my things and store them. I'm sure you won't want to store my stuff. I can't tell you how much I appreciate all you did for me. PS: don't forget those kids at St. Brendan's will still need you. Thanks, Holly

Lukas's fist crumpled the letter. He felt gutted. He felt hollow. He felt sick. His throat was tight. His eyes stung.

So he was wrong again. She didn't love him, after all.

It was the first day of the rest of her life. And then it was the second. And then the third.

But no matter how hard Holly tried, she couldn't seem to live in the moment. She had spent the whole last week of her life in New York out at her mother's on Long Island. She told herself it was the right thing to do. It was what she'd always intended. It didn't have anything to do with leaving Lukas's at the crack of dawn so she wouldn't have to face him in the clear light of day.

She was doing the right thing, she told herself over and over. She was doing what she'd planned—and she was making things easier for Lukas. He might think he wanted to marry her, but he didn't mean it.

He could marry anyone—the remarkable, sophisticated, elegant Grace Marchand, for example. If he didn't want to marry a paragon like Grace, he certainly wouldn't want to marry her! She told herself that every day, too. And by the end of the week at her mother's, she had done a reasonably good job of convincing herself that was the truth. Besides, she was eager to get to Hawaii. That was something else she repeated again and again.

Her mother wasn't convinced. She looked worried every time she glanced Holly's way. "Are you sure you're all right?" she asked Holly.

"I'm fine," Holly assured her.

"Because you don't look very happy."

"I'm happy," Holly lied.

She would be—in time. It would be a relief when she got to Hawaii and started her training. She just needed something new and different—a new challenge to find herself.

Hawaii was different. All balmy breezes and sunshine. And the training was thorough and demanding and thought-provoking. Or it would have been, Holly was sure, if she'd been thinking about it. She didn't.

She thought about Lukas.

She showed up dutifully to every talk and had a hard
time paying attention to a word that was said. In her mind,
she kept seeing Lukas. She went to language classes and
practiced and found herself wondering which ancient languages Lukas knew. She remembered the night of her
prom when he'd confessed he liked studying Latin. She
knew he even translated old documents sometimes.

"To keep my hand in," he'd said, then added wryly,
"And my brain."

It had prompted her once to look him up in some schol-
arly indexes and she'd discovered he was there, that while
he'd been out digging in the dirt with Skeet, he'd spent his
evenings on ancient Sanskrit and Greek texts.

Every evening they prepared and ate local foods from
the island she would be going to. It was a new program,
an attempt to get them acclimated, to help them land on
their feet. And while it was interesting and she learned
it, it didn't stir her blood the way watching Lukas in the
kitchen had.

Her mouth watered when she thought about the spaghetti he'd made. He had half a dozen recipes he'd got
from his mother and grandmother that he had fixed for
her, too. "You don't have to do all the cooking," he'd told
her. "Or we can do it together. Then we can do this while
we're waiting for the water to boil," he'd said with one of
his lopsided grins. And then he'd kissed her.

She ached remembering how Lukas had used almost
any excuse to kiss her. She ached remembering the feel
of his silky hair beneath her fingers, his rough, whiskered
jaw rubbing against her cheek. She ached whenever she
thought about the way he always knew where to touch
her—and how he could let go and allow her to learn what
pleased him.

"Don't think about it. Forget him," she said over and

over. But she couldn't stop thinking about it. And she feared she would never forget this past month as long as she lived.

She went through the motions of the program day after day. She attended the lectures, practiced the language, learned new skills. She tried to fill the emptiness in her life with what she was learning now, what she was planning to do.

And at night when the other volunteers were drinking beer, laughing and talking and making plans, Holly walked on the beach alone.

It had seemed a brilliant idea last autumn when she'd looked into the project in the first place. But then she had finally come to terms with what had happened and had been trying to redefine her life after losing Matt. The Peace Corps had seemed to offer exactly what she needed to challenge herself, to do some good while finding out who she was and what she wanted to do with the rest of her life. It had been a good idea at the time.

Now it was too late.

Because she was, heaven help her, in love with Lukas Antonides. And all the lectures and language lessons and attempts to cook mysterious foods could not fill the hole that leaving him had opened in her life.

This wasn't like the hole Matt had left. His death had brought an irrevocable end to life as she had known it. And she'd had to face that there was no way to change it, no possibility to bring him back. She'd had to face that— and learn to move on.

But Lukas hadn't died. He hadn't left her.

She had left him.

Lukas had said he loved her. Had always loved her. The words echoed in her mind as she stood and stared out at the setting sun. Lukas had asked her to marry him.

190 THE RETURN OF ANTONIDES

And she had been afraid to.

Holly wasn't sure the exact moment she faced the truth—which wasn't that Lukas didn't love her, but that she was afraid to love him. She was afraid to open her heart, to risk the pain of loving again.

But it was too late to protect herself.

She already did.

Charlotte spun slowly around the cavernous space on the gallery's fourth floor and said, "It's getting very airy in here."

Lukas, halfway through knocking down another brick wall, merely grunted and kept on working, first with a crowbar, then a hammer and chisel. He wasn't knocking down any more walls than he and Alex had agreed on. Well, maybe a couple more, but it was his building, damn it. And he needed the exertion if he was going to stay sane. He'd thought about going back to Australia and digging again. He'd stayed because he had made commitments. No one could say he wasn't reliable, he thought grimly.

Charlotte stopped spinning and came over to peer closely at him. "Are you sure you're okay, Lukas?"

"I'm fine," he said shortly. They were all fussing at him. He knew they were concerned. He'd never thought he was the sort of guy who wore his heart on his sleeve, but they all knew he was pining for Holly. It was embarrassing. But he endured it. What else could he do?

Someday, he figured, he'd even get over it. Though since he'd carried a torch for her for two thirds of his life already, he wasn't going to hold his breath.

"A bunch of us are going out for pizza in about an hour," Charlotte said when he stopped hammering. "Want to come with us?"

Lukas shook his head. "No." Then, realizing how abrupt that was, he grimaced and added, "Thanks. Not hungry." He kept moving the chisel, whacking it with the hammer, moving it again. Each blow sent pieces of brick scattering to the canvas tarps below. Lukas wiped a weary forearm across his brow.

"You have to eat," Charlotte reminded him. "You're getting skinny," she said, assessing his shirtless frame.

"I eat."

Tallie saw to that. She kept bringing him food and inviting him for dinner. Ever since she and Elias had discovered that Holly had left, they'd been hovering like worried parents.

"Tallie left me, too," Elias reminded him. "Took me months to find her."

"I know where Holly is," Lukas said stonily.

"So go and get her," his brother said bluntly.

Lukas just shook his head. He couldn't tell them that Holly wouldn't welcome him if he did, that she didn't want him, didn't love him, that it had only been an affair to her.

"If we can do anything..." Tallie said, putting a hand on his arm as they were leaving. "If you want to talk..."

He didn't want to talk. For once in his life Lukas had absolutely nothing to say.

He stonewalled his family. He stonewalled Sera, who fretted about him whenever she came into his office and found him staring into space. He stonewalled Charlotte and the rest of the artists who kept trying to find helpful ways for him to convince Holly to come back and be the business manager again. He didn't tell them he figured she'd probably be happy to remain as the business manager if only he would go away.

Thinking about it now, his throat got tight. It wasn't

the thinking that did it. It was because he was knocking down walls and there was dust everywhere. Too much damn dust.

"If you change your mind, we're leaving sixish," Charlotte said, then headed toward the door. "Leave a wall or two standing," she added. "We don't want the world to come crashing down."

God no, Lukas thought grimly, *we certainly don't want that.*

Charlotte had barely disappeared when his cell phone vibrated in his pocket. It would be Tallie telling him to come for dinner. He dug into his pocket, already deciding that he wasn't going over there tonight. Enough was enough. But it was Sera's name on the caller ID.

"I thought you'd gone home," he said when he answered.

"I was just leaving when someone came in who wants to apply for a MacClintock grant."

Lukas groaned. "We're done with that."

"For next year," Sera qualified. He could hear the smile in her voice. She knew he was so relieved to have it over for the year that she could tease a bit.

But Lukas had had enough of grant applicants for a while. "Tell him to come back next year."

Sera didn't say anything. She had learned by now that if she wanted something, she could always wait him out.

Lukas sighed. "Oh, hell, fine. Send him up. I'll discourage him myself." Or maybe he could kick the guy in the butt, give him some gumption like Skeet wanted.

Because look where gumption got you, Lukas thought bitterly. He, for example, had accomplished so much by laying his heart on the line.

He slid down the ladder at the sound of footsteps on

the stairs and turned to meet the prospective MacClintock applicant.

It wasn't a guy. A slender, dark-haired woman was silhouetted in the late-afternoon sunlight that spilled into the room. Lukas glanced, and felt his heart kick over in his chest because it looked like... But he was dreaming. Had to be. It was a mirage. Like one of those damned oases that tempted camel drivers who had spent too long in the desert.

And then she came toward him.

"Holly?" Lukas dropped the hammer on his foot.

"Lukas! Oh, God, are you all right?" Holly didn't have time to stop and drink in the sight of him, didn't, in the end, worry that he would take one look and tell her to get the hell out of his life.

Once she saw the hammer fall and saw Lukas wince with pain, all her own misgivings fled. She dashed across the room to kneel at his feet.

"Sit down!" she demanded, tugging at the hem of his faded denim jeans. She shoved the offending hammer away and tugged again, and finally Lukas sat. She fumbled off his work boot and sock to find a goose egg forming on the top of his foot. "We need to get ice on it."

"No," Lukas said. "We don't." And his hands grabbed her upper arms and held her still. His Adam's apple worked in his throat. "We need to know what you're doing here, Holly. *I* need to know." His eyes bored into hers.

And Holly knew she couldn't deflect the question. She smiled a little wryly. "Sera told you," she said softly. "I want to apply for a grant."

Lukas cocked his head. A tiny line appeared between his brows. "What're you talking about?"

Holly licked her lips. "Courage," she said, meeting his

gaze, feeling herself drowning in those green depths. "I need some."

Lukas's expression seemed to close up. His jaw tightened. He looked away. "For the Peace Corps?" he said tonelessly. He didn't look at her. He was staring away across the room, as if looking at her would hurt.

Holly knew the feeling. She lifted a hand, wanting to touch him, to draw strength from him, then knew she couldn't. She had to do this on her own. "No," she said. "To tell you I love you, too."

Lukas's gaze snapped back to lock onto hers. "You—?" There was green fire in his gaze now, and hope in his eyes. "Holly?" His voice seemed to break.

Holly wetted her lips and nodded, then said them again. "I love you, Lukas. I do. I...didn't want to. I was afraid to."

"Afraid?" He sounded aghast. "I would never hurt you!" Then he had the grace to look abashed. "Once I did," he admitted. "Probably more than once, but I swear I won't anymore. Not ever. Not if I can help it," he added wryly. "I'm not very good at this."

Holly shook her head. She took his hands in hers, felt his fingers tighten around them. "You're very good at it," she said, and meant it. Once she'd allowed herself to believe what Lukas had told her, she realized how much effort he had made on her behalf. "I'm the one who's not," she admitted. "I'm the one who didn't trust. I told myself it was because you couldn't be trusted—"

"Imagine that," Lukas said wryly, but he was smiling now.

"But it wasn't you. It was me. I didn't trust myself to believe. I didn't think I had enough to make you happy. To keep you."

"For God's sake, Hol'!" he protested. "You've had me from the day you fell out of that damn tree!"

She laughed. "You wanted to throttle me!"

"Because I was eleven. When you're eleven that's what you do."

"Really?"

He nodded. "I think deep down, I've loved you for years."

Holly lowered her eyes, looked at their clasped hands, then raised her gaze again to meet his. "I loved you, too." She swallowed, then tried to explain. "I loved both of you. You were so different. He was warm, steady, constant, responsible."

"And I was not," Lukas said frankly, giving a rough laugh.

"You were…scary." She loosed one of her hands, lifting it to touch his cheek. "I never knew where I stood with you."

"In my heart."

Holly blinked at the prompt certainty of his response. "You had a funny way of showing it. Pulling pigtails. Trying to run off. Teasing."

"Like I said, I was eleven. I didn't do hearts and flowers. And by the time I woke up to what I should be doing," he said ruefully, "Matt already was."

Holly nodded. Neither of them spoke for a long moment, both of them, she was sure, thinking about Matt. "He kept me safe," she told Lukas.

"I know. He was the better man."

"No," Holly said quickly. "He was no more perfect than you are, than I am. And," she admitted for the first time, "you might have been right that we were too young to get engaged—"

"I wanted you for myself," Lukas told her. "I didn't deliberately mean to hurt you that night. I wanted you to give him up, pick me instead." He shook his head. "Thank

God you didn't. I wasn't mature enough to get married then. Matt was."

"He was the right man for me at that time."

Lukas nodded. "Yes." He took her hand. He ran his fingers over it, then clasped it in his, firm and strong. He didn't say a word, just looked at her. Holly knew what he was asking. She could see his heart in his eyes.

"I don't need a grant," she told him. "You've given me the courage. I'm still scared—not that you don't love me, but that I'll lose you, too."

"No! I promise—"

She touched his lips with her fingers. "You can only promise to love me, Lukas, as I promise to love you. That's all we can do." She gave him a tremulous smile. "So. If you're still offering, I'd love to marry you, Lukas Antonides."

He took her into his arms before the words were out of her mouth. His kiss was fierce and possessive, and Holly met him with a desperation all her own. He got brick dust all over her—on her clothes, on her face, in her hair. He might have got it in far more scandalous places, but as he was sliding his hands up under her shirt, she shifted to give him more access and accidentally kicked his injured foot.

Lukas winced.

Holly felt sanity returning, at least momentarily.

"Up," Holly insisted, standing, then hauling a limping Lukas to his feet. "You need ice, compression, rest, elevation."

"Bed," Lukas translated, grinning. He looped an arm over Holly's shoulders, then lifted a hopeful brow as she helped him hobble toward the stairs. "You are the best thing that ever happened to me, Hol'. I love you."

Holly went up on her toes and brushed her lips against

Lukas's. "I love you, too." It still scared her. But not as much as being without him did. "And yes, my love," she said with an impish smile, "a bed sounds like a great idea. I think we can arrange that."

* * * * *

Amanda Cinelli

———

Christmas at the Castello

'THERE'S STILL SOMETHING MISSING.'

Dara stood poised at the top of the staircase, looking over the Winter Wonderland theme that had transformed the opulent grand ballroom below her. Her assistant, Mia, waited patiently by her side. The younger woman had long ago got used to her boss's obsessive eye for detail. Devlin Events was about creating perfect Sicilian weddings for their high-profile clients. Over the past three years Dara had gained an army of the industry's most talented people and put them onto her payroll, but she still liked to oversee the final run-throughs at their most prominent venues. There was no one in the industry who could spot the little things better than she. And right now something was off.

Sweeping yet another glance around the room, she mentally checked off twenty-five tables, each adorned with a glittering crystal tree centrepiece. The overall effect was like a winter forest, with white and blue lighting completing the wintry theme. Her bride, a famous opera singer, had expressly forbidden any real flower arrangements on the tables. She had instead ordered hundreds of spherical arrangements of fresh white and pink roses, to be suspended from the ceiling in intricately symmetrical clusters.

Dara counted across the floating flower bombs—as she had so lovingly named them. She got as far as the third row before she noticed the problem.

She sighed. 'They've doubled up on the colours.'

Mia's head snapped up. 'Are you sure?'

'Right over here.'

She walked down the marble staircase, the click of her heels echoing on the hard surface. She came to a stop underneath the offending decoration. It wasn't a major issue, but it was damned irritating now she'd noticed it. Mia's quiet voice came from behind her.

'Should I fetch one of the guys from the ceremony room?'

Dara shook her head. 'The wedding is due to start in two hours—the ceremony room is priority.' She smoothed down the front of her sleek red pencil skirt, trying to focus on everything *but* the mismatched flowers above her. Her eyes drifted upwards again.

Mia laughed. 'I'll go and get somebody.'

She disappeared out through the door, leaving Dara alone in the glittering winter ballroom.

The rest of the room was perfect. Her team was talented, and very capable of doing most of the work unchaperoned. She could pick and choose which events to attend, leaving her plenty of time to travel with her jet-setting husband. But it had been three weeks since she and Leo had been together—his newest business expansion into Asia had kept him away much longer than usual.

The restlessness that had plagued her over the past months seemed to have intensified in the absence of her husband. Three weeks was the longest they had spent apart. She was unable to shake the feeling that something was wrong—or perhaps something was about to *go* wrong.

Their joint venture into charity work in Sicily kept her busy. The Valente Foundation was doing fantastic work in some of the most disadvantaged areas on the island. And with Christmas fast approaching there was lots of volun-

teer work to do. But, as busy as she kept herself, something
still kept her wide awake at night and staring at the ceiling.

Making a snap decision, she grabbed a ladder from
nearby and set it up, removing her heels in the process.
She didn't need to stand here waiting for a big strong man
to fix the problem. There was no reason why she couldn't
do it herself.

She quickly reached the top, keeping both hands in
front of her on the cold metal for balance. It was true: if
you wanted a job done well, sometimes you had to do it
yourself. She focused on the arrangement, unhooking it
from its place and lowering it down. It was heavier than
she had expected, and she gasped as the world unexpect-
edly tilted on its axis.

'*Dio*, what *is* it with you and ladders?' a deep voice
shouted from below her as the ladder suddenly righted itself and she was entirely vertical again.

'Leo.' Her heart gave a sharp thump.

Her husband was looking up at her, his hands holding
the metal ladder steady. Dara dropped the flower arrangement and cursed.

'It's nice to see you still haven't lost your love of daring stunts, *carina*.'

Dara descended the ladder as quickly as she could
manage and practically fell into her husband's arms. The
familiar smell of him surrounded her, making her sigh
involuntarily.

'Surprise…' he whispered huskily against her neck.

His permanent five o'clock shadow brushed against
her skin and she shivered. Oh, how she had missed those
shivers.

'You're a week early.' She pulled back in his arms.

He smirked. 'I like to be unpredictable.'

She loved it when he smiled like that, filled with mischief. Life was too serious without Leo around.

'I've got a surprise planned. Do you think you can manage a few days away from your work?'

'Right *now*? Leo, that sounds wonderful, but I'm needed here.'

Dara made a noise of protest, only to have him silence her with a finger against her lips.

'Do you remember your wedding vows, Signora Valente?'

Dara remembered their wedding day as if it had been yesterday. She had originally planned a simple ceremony on the beach in the Caribbean. But then they'd both realised there was only one place they could imagine becoming man and wife, attended by a few select family and friends: the *castello*, which had become the setting for the most romantic day of her life.

'We both agreed to remove that medieval part about obeying one's husband from our vows.' She raised a brow.

'I'm talking about the part where we promised to spend each and every day loving each other.' His gaze darkened as his hand drifted lower on her back. 'And it seems I've got about twenty-two days of loving to make up for.'

His mouth lowered to hers and captured it in a scorching kiss full of dark, sensual promise.

A muted cough interrupted them from their interlude. Mia, accompanied by one of the movers, stood awkwardly at the top of the stairs. Dara stood back from their sensual embrace, her cheeks flaming.

'Nice to see you home safe, Mr Valente,' Mia said and blushed. 'Shall I book you both into the restaurant for lunch?'

'I've come to steal my wife away, I'm afraid.'

Dara placed a hand against her chest, straightening her

blazer as casually as she could manage under the scrutiny of her staff. 'Leo, I can't just leave two hours before an event—'

'Actually, you can,' Mia interrupted, blushing even more as both Leo and Dara turned to face her. 'What I mean is, Dara, you've been working so hard… What's the point in being the boss if you can't take some time off? The rest of the team can see this through perfectly well.'

Leo moved forward, grabbing Dara's shoes from the floor. 'Mia, you are the voice of reason.'

Dara shook her head, smiling. 'This is crazy. I have a million things I should be doing.'

'That's what makes stealing you away so much fun.' He winked, pulling her by the hand. 'Mia, you are only to call my wife if there is a fire or some other catastrophic event.'

'Understood, sir.' The assistant saluted, giggling uncontrollably as Leo commandeered his speechless wife from the room in her bare feet.

'Is the blindfold really necessary?' Dara asked, feeling for Leo's hand in the close confines of his sleek sports car.

'Necessary? Perhaps not,' Leo's voice purred silkily somewhere next to her ear. 'But it adds to my enjoyment.'

Dara reached out, her hand coming into contact with his arm: a band of hard muscle covered in the rich silk of his dark shirt. 'Well, in two years of marriage you've never mentioned this particular fantasy.'

Dara's breath whooshed out of her lungs as a warm hand settled possessively upon her inner thigh. It had been weeks since she'd felt her husband's hands on her body, and the sensation was just as addictive as she remembered.

'I've never been one for power plays, but I must say I am enjoying the effect so far,' he murmured seductively.

'I'm open to the blindfold, but I'm drawing the line at

handcuffs,' she replied, focusing on the agonising slowness of his fingers as they progressed towards the hem of her skirt.

'We're hot enough in the bedroom without adding props, *carina*,' he rasped, gripping her thigh and squeezing gently. 'And I'm liable to stop this car on the side of the road if you don't stop making those delicious little noises.'

Dara smiled to herself, hearing his laboured breathing. 'I'll behave myself if it means avoiding an accident. Still, I'm not opposed to you being so out of control.'

He chuckled. 'I'll make note of that.'

Less than fifteen minutes later the car had moved off the motorway and onto rougher terrain. She had expected him to take her to the private airfield where they normally housed the jet, but he wouldn't have needed to blindfold her for that. The past Christmases of their relationship had been spent travelling abroad. Sipping champagne at the top of the Eiffel Tower…exploring deserted beaches in Bali. She wondered what on earth he had planned this year. Curiosity made her stomach jolt with excitement as she felt the car suddenly pull to a smooth stop.

Leo jumped out from the car, ordering her to wait as he opened her door and helped her out into the crisp night air. He gently removed the blindfold, allowing Dara a moment as her eyes adjusted to her surroundings.

She looked up at the familiar facade of Castello Bellamo and felt her breath catch. Thousands of tiny twinkling fairy lights adorned the steps to the double doors. The entrance glowed as though lit up by some kind of magical force.

'The real surprise is inside.' Leo took her by the hand and led her up the steps and through the open doors into the grand hallway.

The *castello* had always been a magical place to her,

with its vaulted ceilings and mysterious corridors. But now it simply took her breath away. Thick garlands of flowers adorned each side of the staircase, and tiny ornamental elves sat on a side table surrounded by candlelight. The light from the chandelier above had been left dimmed for maximum effect, and she could see a warm glow emanating from the doorway leading into the front sitting room.

'Leo, the place looks like something from a fairy tale.' She sighed, wandering through the archway. Her breath caught as she took in the enormous Christmas tree that dominated the room. The tree had to be at least nine feet tall, and was perfectly decorated in an array of red and gold. 'Did you do this all by yourself?' she asked, still stunned by all the effort he'd gone to.

'I had some help,' he admitted. 'I remembered you spoke about how much you loved the traditional family Christmases you had as a child.' Moving his weight onto one foot, he leaned against the archway and watched her. 'Do you like it?'

Dara turned to him, feeling tears well up in her eyes as she realised that her powerful jet-setting husband was actually nervous.

'Leo, this is so thoughtful, I'm actually—' She swallowed down her emotion, trying not to ruin the moment with silly tears.

'What's wrong? Have I upset you?' Leo was by her side in an instant and enveloping her into his strong embrace. 'I know that we usually spend this time of year somewhere warmer and more exotic. Are you disappointed?'

Dara shook her head quickly, looking up into the brilliant emerald depths of his eyes. He was so serious, so concerned, and yet she couldn't seem to find the words to assure him that this was wonderful.

'It's perfect,' she rasped. 'Thank you.'

She felt his arms relax around her, pulling her closer into the wall of his chest. She tilted her head up and claimed his mouth in a kiss full of heat and promise.

Leo groaned and smoothed his hands down Dara's back slowly, allowing his hands to rest on her supple curves. She was still as addictive as ever, his wife. And he'd be damned, but he couldn't wait another moment before having her.

The soft rug before the fire made for an excellent makeshift bed. He lowered them both to the floor slowly, unbuttoning his shirt in the process. Dara began to pull at the buttons on her own blouse, but Leo had other plans. He laid a hand gently on top of hers.

'I've been fantasizing for weeks about undressing you,' he whispered sensuously as he ran a slow, torturous hand down her ribcage.

Dara shivered, heat rising in her cheeks. 'You still fantasize about me?' She looked doubtful.

'*Amore mio*, you are the only woman who gets me like this. Look at me—I'm rock-hard and struggling for breath after one kiss.'

Dara's eyes sparked with possession as she laid her hand on his belt buckle. 'I'm glad. Because I plan on being the only woman for a long time yet.'

Leo sucked in a breath as her fingers undid the buckle, lowering the zip of his trousers in one smooth movement. Her hand wandered, momentarily grazing his erection and making him groan.

'Such a tease,' he growled, pushing her back down onto the rug. 'This is *my* fantasy, remember?'

Leo grabbed the waistline of her pencil skirt, tugging it low on her hips before removing it completely. What he saw beneath made his eyes widen and his heart thump uncomfortably. Delicate thigh-high stockings covered her legs, held in place by a black lace garter belt.

'This is new.' He felt his throat run dry.

Dara's blush deepened. 'I had a feeling you'd like it.'

Leo ran his hand across the flimsy lace, feeling the heat of her skin underneath. A matching thong was the only thing that lay between his fingers and the moist heat of her delicate skin beneath.

'I planned to take my time…' He bit his lower lip, watching her eyes darken as she arched her hips against his hand. He leaned down, taking the lace between his teeth as he undid one catch and rolled the stocking slowly down the smooth skin of her thigh. Discarding it on the floor, he turned his attention to the other thigh and repeated the action. Dara shivered, unconsciously spreading her thighs wide for him. Or maybe it wasn't unconscious at all; maybe she was deliberately trying to drive him insane.

Pushing the thin lace to one side, Leo trailed one fingertip along the slick crease between her thighs. Dara moaned under his touch, pressing closer into his hand. He could tell that she was ready for him. But a wicked part of him made her wait a moment longer. He leaned just close enough to blow a single breath of hot air against her sensitive flesh.

Dara gasped, gripping the hair at the nape of his neck to pull him closer.

The action drove him wild. She was flushed and breathing harshly. Leo obeyed her breathless plea, pressing his lips to her tender flesh and hearing her groan in response. He moved his mouth in sync with his fingers, driving her closer and closer to that point of no return. He felt her body tense under the onslaught of pleasure. A single curse escaped those delicate lips as she reached her climax.

No sooner had her aftershocks subsided than he was thrusting deep inside her, sinking into her molten heat with a muttered curse of his own. 'Oh, *Dio*, I've missed this.' He groaned as he built up a steady rhythm, spreading her legs wide as he leaned down and took one taut nipple into his mouth.

Dara caressed his back with her fingertips as he drove into her with all the control he could muster.

His release came hard and fast, taking them both by surprise.

Once the wave of pleasure had subsided, he sank down on the rug by her side and exhaled hard.

Dara sat up on one elbow, tracing the hairs on his chest idly. 'That was worth the wait.'

Leo murmured his agreement, feeling her hands on his chest and listening to her rhythmic breathing as his eyes closed.

Dara couldn't sleep. She stared up at the two stockings that hung over the fireplace. They looked so plain, so small on that huge mantelpiece. That same feeling that had plagued her for the past few months threatened to overcome her again.

This wasn't about the stockings.

The same way as her frequent trips to Syracuse had nothing at all to do with business.

Since they had opened up their charitable project, the Valente Foundation, she had been required to attend a handful of fundraisers and benefits. Her presence wasn't necessarily required in any of the institutions they supported on a day-to-day basis, and yet she had found herself taking on the role of patroness at the Syracuse orphanage with the aim of being a silent figure.

The first couple of trips had been to check on the progress of some renovations, and then she had arranged for a new playground to be built. That playground had been finished in the summer, and yet she still found reason to visit as often as she could manage. With Leo away she had found herself making the hour-long trip up to three times a week. Even the ever-smiling house matron had begun to look confused at her continued presence.

There were stockings up on the fireplace at the orphanage too. Seventeen of them, side by side, hanging on a string in the common room. Now that Leo was home she supposed she would find no reason to go to Syracuse again. He would ask questions about why she visited only one orphanage—why not all the others? Why not the hospitals? He would know, just as she knew, that her actions weren't about being charitable at all.

The press had been merciless in the beginning: everyone had wanted to see Leo Valente transformed from playboy to father. Dara had never made a secret of her inability to bear children, so it had been no surprise that the press had caught wind of it soon after their wedding. The rumour mill had gone into overdrive. Would they adopt? Would they use a surrogate? They'd been a hot topic for quite some time.

They had decided that their business was their own, and that their choice to remain childless was both private and definite.

Hot tears threatened to fall from her eyes now, as emotion built in her throat. It just didn't make sense. She had made it clear from the start—before they married—that children were not in her future. She'd made her peace with that on a hospital bed, upon being informed that her condition was incurable. She hadn't been foolish enough to hold out any hope of some day carrying a child of her own. It was better to be realistic. She had never had strong maternal tendencies anyway. For goodness' sake, she was a workaholic and a complete neat freak—both qualities didn't exactly mix well with motherhood.

She knew all this and yet she had been selfish enough to go back to the orphanage after that first time. Selfish and inconsiderate.

She had been plagued by a sense of restlessness these past few months. Married life was wonderful, and her success in her career was at an all-time high. And yet it seemed as if the only time she felt whole these days was when she was there.

The children were wonderfully well behaved, thanks to the efforts of the brilliant schoolteachers led by Matron Anna. Each visit brought with it new adventures filled with laughter. Life was less serious, less stressful.

A vision of small brown eyes and a playful grin filled her mind. A small hand holding on to hers so tightly. She couldn't keep lying to herself. There was only one reason why she kept going back there, and that reason had a mischievous smile and liked to curl up on her lap to read.

She heard the sounds of Leo waking up behind her and tried to wipe away the tears from her cheeks without him noticing. Tried and failed.

'Dara?' He was up in an instant, sleep clouding his eyes. 'Has something happened?'

'I'm fine—let's just go up to bed.' She shook off his embrace, pulling a blanket from the sofa to drape around her shoulders.

'You've been crying.'

'I'm fine…honestly.' She tried to avoid his penetrating gaze, turning to poke at the dwindling embers in the grate.

'You've been acting strangely since we got here. I thought you loved this place—I thought being here on a more permanent basis would make you happy.'

'It does. I'm looking forward to us spending Christmas here together.'

'Dara, I don't know what is going on with you. You've been avoiding some of my phone calls while I was away. Even when I specifically called when I knew you'd be finished with work. And today my driver mentioned that you've been disappearing by yourself for hours at a time. With no reasonable explanation—'

'You had your driver keeping tabs on me?' Dara was incredulous.

'I wasn't going to pay it any attention, because I trust you. But dammit, Dara, you're hiding something from me and I want to know what it is. *Now.*'

'What do you think? That I'm cheating on you?'

Leo crossed his arms, looking darkly into the glowing fire. 'I'd like to think I know you better than that.'

Dara placed her hands on her hips. 'Well, it sounds like you're accusing me of something. I'm entitled to *some* level of privacy. Just because we're married, it doesn't mean we need to live in each other's pockets, for goodness' sake.'

She moved to walk away and felt his hand move gently to her wrist.

'Dara…'

His voice was quiet, and something in its tone appealed to her logic. She knew she was behaving out of character. And that he must be concerned. He had flown for almost twenty-four hours to come here and surprise her, and here she was shouting at him for asking if she was okay.

The realisation brought even more tears.

'I'm sorry.'

She sat down heavily on the sofa, hiding her face in her hands. She felt him come to her, felt his solid warmth slide alongside her and envelop her as she sat there trying to make sense of why she was falling apart.

'I've been going to the orphanage in Syracuse,' she admitted. 'It started as a simple project to update their facilities. But then it became…more.'

Leo sat silently, watching her reveal her secrets.

'I was there one day, helping to choose wallpaper for the common room, when one of the smallest children—a boy—walked right up to me and grabbed my hand. The other children had avoided me on previous visits; I was a stranger with a foreign accent and a fancy suit. I was unapproachable.' She smiled to herself. 'But not him. He grabbed on to my hand and asked me to come and see his drawings. He had drawn a picture of a house by the sea. He gave it to me as a gift and asked me if I would come back again. So I did.'

Leo remained silent for a moment, watching her. 'Why do you feel the need to hide all this? It's charitable work.'

'Don't you see? It's *not* work to me. I *want* to be there. It makes me happy to be there with all the children. But most of all with Luca…'

'Luca is the boy's name?' Leo asked quietly.

Dara nodded. 'It's unfair of me to grow attached. Because he's just a child and he will think that I want to… that we might want to…' The words stuck in her throat, unable to come out.

'That you might want to become his mother?' Leo said.

Dara looked at him quickly, as though he had struck her. That one word was enough to make her mind turn to panic. *Mother.*

'I won't go back again. I suppose I'm only just realizing that I've used the orphanage to relieve my restlessness. To occupy myself.'

She stood up and walked to the Christmas tree, touching one of the golden baubles and making it spin.

'It was a selfish act and I'm feeling guilty, that's all.'

Dara turned back to her husband. He sat completely
nude on the sofa, watching her with a look so concerned
it melted her heart. If she told him any more she would
only regret it in the morning. It wasn't that she feared his
judgement. In fact it was completely the opposite. She
feared his pity.

Leo had taken the news of her infertility in his stride
from the moment she'd revealed her secret to him. He had
been understanding, and he had helped her to realize that
her condition did not define her.

To bring up all those old insecurities now would only
belittle how far they had come as a couple.

That was the thing, though—she wasn't quite so confident that she had ever rid herself of them at all. Rather,
she had just chosen to focus on being the beautiful woman
that Leo made her feel she was and ignored the sad and
broken woman of her past.

She bit her lip. Leo was looking at her intensely, waiting for her to speak. She couldn't tell him the truth, not
tonight anyway.

'I'm sorry. I feel like I've ruined this wonderful night
with my own silly ramblings.' She shook her head, banishing the dark thoughts from her mind.

She walked to him and straddled his lap.

'Dara, we're having quite a serious conversation here,
and I will find it very difficult to concentrate with you in
this position.'

He shifted, but she moulded her body even closer to
him.

'I've had enough talking for tonight.' She leaned over
him, nipping his earlobe just hard enough to make him
groan. 'You said we have twenty-two days to make up for,
and I plan on obeying my husband's wishes.'

She smiled wickedly, banishing all other thoughts from their minds as their bodies instinctively moved against each other.

Leo sat on the terrace, looking out at the midday winter sun shining on the choppy waves of the bay. Most of their morning had been spent in bed, making up for lost time. But some time after brunch Dara had found herself taking a call from Mia about something vitally important. Rather than being annoyed at the interruption, Leo had once again been impressed at how much his wife's company relied on her.

She ran Devlin Events like a well-oiled machine—just as he would expect. But still her staff looked to her for guidance, and felt comfortable in doing so. This was one of the main reasons for her skyrocketing success. Her employees were satisfied, and therefore so were her clients. Add that to the fact that she was unbelievably talented and passionate, and it could only be a recipe for success.

He watched her through the terrace doors as she booted up her tablet computer and wielded it like a clipboard. She was tense, even after a night of being thoroughly made love to.

Her revelation about her trips to the orphanage had confused him. Dara had never shown any interest in children. He had never even seen her speak to a child, not to mention drive out of her way to go and visit one. But recently he had begun to feel a distance between them. They both had busy careers, but they usually made sure to keep time for each other.

Leo stood, suddenly needing to walk. He took the path down along the cliff-face—the same path he'd used to take as a boy. He stopped on the flight of steps that led down to the old boathouse, remembering his childhood self rushing

down the stone steps, furiously trying to hold in the tears
and escape his nightmarish life. Living with a mentally
ill mother had forced him to live in silence. His formative
years had been spent in isolation, and in fear of upsetting
her with his mere presence.

Those memories no longer held the same dark power
over him—not since Dara had come into his life. Now
every time he walked down here he was reminded that
he was happier than either of his parents had ever been.

Right now, he was impressed that the little boathouse
was still standing. He pushed the door open with a creak
and ducked his head inside.

A row of plastic boxes lined the floor—he had insu-
lated the place last year, once they had decided to use it
for storage rather than leave it to rot. Flipping the lid of the
box nearest the window, Leo idly surveyed the contents. A
collection of coloured yo-yos lay inside, once his favourite
boyhood hobby. He picked up a red one and spun the yarn
tightly between the circular wooden discs.

He had spent many days inside these four walls, prac-
tising his skills and hoping for someone to show them to.
He held the yo-yo tight in his hand before letting it fall to
the ground and bouncing it back up easily. His tricks had
been numerous, all learned from a book he had got as a
gift from his father. He knew now that his father's secretary had probably chosen it, but at the time he had taken
it as a challenge to impress the old man. And, as he did
with most tasks, he'd poured his heart and soul into it.

In a way he was no different from the little boy who
had captured his wife's attention. Leo might not have been
an orphan, but he knew what it meant to crave a connection. He had that with Dara now—he felt the completeness that came from the love of a good woman. He had

poured all his efforts into creating a life together with his beautiful wife.

Since meeting Dara he had slowly lost interest in the party scene—except for when he opened up a new club. As a bachelor, he had spent his leisure time mainly involved in drinking too much and buying the fastest cars. He'd had no difficulty living in hotels for months at a time. He hadn't known what it meant to have a home.

Dara had shown him just how fulfilling life could be. But now he got the feeling that she felt their life was lacking somehow. If she was happy, why was she escaping to Syracuse every chance she could get?

An image of the longing in her eyes when she spoke about the child there filled his mind. It was suddenly blindingly clear that Dara had developed a newfound yearning for motherhood. And somehow that yearning wasn't something she felt comfortable sharing with him. The thought jarred him, leaving an uncomfortable knot in his stomach.

Leo ran a hand through his hair and threw the yo-yo back into the box. He had never once questioned Dara's steadfast opinion on family. She had made it clear that she would never have children, and that had suited them both. The idea of fatherhood had never been something he aspired to. His own father had been a spectre in his life—one who had drifted in and out, leaving him uncertain and confused. As an adult he had never once considered the idea of starting a family of his own.

But lately he had begun to grow tired of the constant travelling. These days the only place he wanted to be was here, with his wife, in their true home. He had wanted to say that to her last night, but they had got sidetracked.

He walked back to the *castello* just as evening was setting in and found Dara waiting for him in the kitchen. A bottle of vintage Prosecco sat on the table, two glasses beside it.

'I'm sorry I took so long.' She winced, pouring him a generous glass of wine.

Leo took a sip, appreciating the taste for a moment before shrugging. 'You have a business to run, *carina*. I have to accept that I can never have you all to myself.'

'I've turned my phone off for the evening, so I am one hundred per cent yours. No distractions.' She smiled, pressing her mouth to his.

Leo held her at arm's length, noticing the shadows under her eyes. 'Good. Because I'd like to continue our discussion from last night.'

Dara removed herself from his arms, turning to take a long gulp from her own glass. 'I'd rather we just leave that, actually. I must have been overtired and emotional.'

Her laugh didn't fool him. 'Dara, are you unhappy?' he asked, and watched her face snap up with alarm.

'Why on earth would you think that?'

'You seem…unfulfilled, somehow. These trips to Syracuse tell me that perhaps you might have changed your mind about some things.'

Dara looked momentarily miserable, her expression filled with intense sadness before shifting back to a mask of calm. Anyone else might not have noticed, but Leo knew her better than anyone.

'It's nothing that I plan to act on,' she said coldly. 'There's no need for you to worry.'

'Why would I worry? We are husband and wife, Dara. We make these kinds of choices together. Maybe I should go with you to Syracuse so you can help me to understand.'

'That's definitely *not* what I want,' Dara snapped.

'*Per l'amore di Dio.*' Leo sucked in a breath to control

his frustration. 'Dara, for God's sake, what *do* you want?' he shouted harshly, feeling instant remorse as she flinched.

They stood in silence for a moment, toe to toe in the silence of the kitchen.

'I won't be shouted at.' Dara spoke quietly. 'I need some time alone. I'll see you at dinner.'

She practically ran from the room. Ran away from him.

Leo frowned, looking out of the window at the waves crashing against the cliffs. He had lost his temper—but could she blame him? He was her *husband*, and yet she was determined to battle whatever was bothering her alone. He had a right to know what this was about.

Clearly the answer lay in Syracuse. If she wouldn't go with him, then he would have to go alone.

Dara awoke to a note on her pillow from Leo, telling her that he had some business to attend to and that he would return by the afternoon. His words were plain and to the point, with none of the flowery terms of affection that they usually used. She felt a pang of hurt that he hadn't woken her before leaving, and now she faced a day in the *castello* alone with her thoughts.

She had been hostile and unfair last night. And now she had driven a wedge between them. She sighed, falling back onto the soft Egyptian cotton bedspread, and stared up at the ceiling.

It wasn't that she didn't *want* to share her inner turmoil with her husband. She just felt that it was pointless to do so. Yes, she had formed a bond with Luca. Yes, for the first time in her life she had felt the all-encompassing yearning to care for a child as her own. But she would never do it. She would never be so naive as to assume that she was in any way qualified to be a parent. She was a very good wedding planner, and she hoped she was a satisfying wife. But she was not cut out to be somebody's mother.

Her own mother had been warm and caring. She had given up her career in hotel management to stay at home as a full-time parent and had made it clear that she believed all women should do the same. Dara knew that Leo didn't think that way—he went out of his way to promote equality in his company, and often commented on how proud he was of his wife's accomplishments. And yet the image of her mother baking in the kitchen would always be her measure of what a good wife looked like.

She stared out at the waves crashing onto the cliffs below. Why was she having all these thoughts now? She *loved* her life. She had more than most women could dream of.

Needing to escape her overactive thoughts, she walked to the window. The winds were too high today to walk down on the beach, and being outside in the chilly December air wasn't her idea of a relaxing getaway.

It had been Leo's idea to take time off work, and yet here he was abandoning her on their third day. Clearly he was annoyed, and was choosing to punish her.

Her mind wandered back to the orphanage once more. She was restless and annoyed with herself for allowing this charade to go on for so long. It wasn't fair to the little boy or to the hopeful orphanage staff. She needed to explain herself and give them a clear idea that she would no longer be visiting.

She could see Luca one last time.

Before she'd even realized what she was doing, she'd picked up her car keys and was powering up the cobbled driveway in her Porsche. She could be at the orphanage within the hour, and back well before lunchtime. Leo wouldn't even know she'd gone anywhere.

* * *

The familiar white stucco facade of the orphanage was like a balm to the uncomfortable ache in her chest. Dara knocked on the door and stepped back when it swung open to reveal the kind-faced head of the orphanage— Matron Anna.

'Signora Valente, I'm surprised to see you here.' She frowned. 'I thought you were in Palermo this week?'

'What would make you think that?' Dara smiled as she stepped inside and let the younger woman take her jacket.

'Signor Valente said that you were so busy this week…'

'He did? When were you speaking with him?' Dara frowned, just as a roar of laughter came from the nearby common room. A familiar voice drifted down the hallway—a deep male voice filled with mischief and laughter.

Dara moved silently towards the doorway of the common room, her heart hammering uncomfortably in her chest. The children were all gathered in the centre of the room, on the floor, and each of their little faces was beaming up at the man who stood in the centre of their circle. Leo stood poised with a red yo-yo in his hand. His posture was like that of a magician about to wow his crowd.

'And now for my next trick…' he proclaimed, waiting a moment as the children shouted loudly for him to continue. 'This one is called the lindy loop. Are you ready?'

The excitement in the air was palpable, and every eye in the room was trained on Leo as he set the red object on an intricate movement up in the air. The yo-yo caught several times on its string, before spinning up into the air and down to the ground and then landing safely back into its master's hand.

The children clapped loudly, shouting multiple requests for new tricks at their entertainer. Leo was calm and indulgent, chatting easily to the crowd of little people in a way

Dara had never seemed to master. She had spent weeks trying to gain the confidence of these kids, and the most she'd managed had been sharing lunch at the same table.

Luca always stayed by her side, though.

Her thoughts back on the present moment, she suddenly absorbed the fact that her husband was *here*. In the orphanage. He had lied to her, and for that she should be furious.

And yet all she felt was a same sense of anticipation. As if she was hurtling head first down a hill and she had no power to stop it.

As she watched, Luca stepped forward from the crowd of children. His soft black curls were falling forward into his eyes as they always did. He had the kind of unruly hair that refused to behave under the ministrations of any brush. She imagined Leo's hair would be much the same if he let it grow any longer.

Catching her thoughts, she shook her head and watched as her husband sank down to his knees to listen to the young boy whisper something into his ear. Leo listened intently for a moment, before breaking into a huge grin. Luca smiled up at him and they both laughed together at their secret joke.

And Dara felt her heart break completely.

Turning from the door, she walked quickly down the corridor and out to her car. The drive home passed in a blur. Her body felt numb and her insides shook violently.

Once she reached the familiar facade of the *castello*, she walked to the stone wall that overlooked the famous cliffs of Monterocca. And only then did she let the tears come. Great racking sobs escaped her throat and sent violent tremors through her.

It was unthinkably cruel that Leo should look so perfect surrounded by children. The one thing that she could never give him. She wept for the children she would never bear. The children she had denied wanting for so long.

Soon the sound of tyres squealing down the driveway interrupted her silence. Heavy steps were moving fast across the courtyard towards her.

Dara turned just as Leo came to a stop. 'Where have you been?' she asked innocently.

'You know where,' Leo gritted. 'They told me that you arrived and then left—driving like a mad woman.'

'You lied to me,' Dara said, her voice almost a whisper.

'I needed to understand.' He stood with his arms crossed.

'And *do* you? Do you understand now why it was so selfish of me to get so attached?'

'To tell the truth, Dara, no—I don't.' He sighed. 'You keep saying you've been selfish. But I don't understand how you can consider giving your time and attention to those children as selfishness.'

'I wasn't *giving* anything, Leo. I was taking. I got too close. I let Luca get attached to me because it made me feel…needed.' She took a deep shuddering breath, shaking her head at her own foolishness. 'It made me feel like—like I was his mother.' She bit her lip. 'Can't you see how wrong that is? I've given him hope for something that can never happen.'

'What makes you believe that it can never happen, Dara?'

'Look at me, for goodness' sake. I'm a control freak who works crazy hours and spends half the year travelling around the world with my nightclub magnate former playboy husband.'

'That's…quite a mouthful.' Leo's brows rose.

'It's the truth.' She shrugged. 'We're not family people. Aside from the fact that we can never have our own biological children.'

Leo walked past her to the ancient stone boundary wall, leaning over to peer down at the rough sea below them. 'I might be a jet-setting former playboy, but I think I would be ten times the father that mine was.'

Dara froze. 'Leo, I didn't mean that you wouldn't make a great father. Of course you would. You're easy-going and kind. You're reliable and intelligent. You would be amazing.' She shook her head. 'But you're married to *me*.'

'Dara, if it wasn't for you I would still be going through life without a true purpose. Falling in love with you made me realize what is truly important in life. Three years ago if you had told me that I would want to spend the rest of my life living in this castle I would have laughed you out of the room.' He turned to her, taking both of her hands in his. 'But here I am. And this is the only place I want to be.'

'I can't be somebody's mother. I just can't.'

'Dara, did you ever stop and think that maybe it's okay not to be the perfect mother? Sometimes it's okay just to try your best. I mean, you're telling me that you're a workaholic, and yet the matron told me that you've been visiting the orphanage three times a week. That's a two-hour round trip, alone, while simultaneously running your own business, yes?'

Dara shrugged. 'I made the time.'

'Exactly. Because you care about this boy.' Leo stepped forward, grasping her hands in his. 'Dara, I went to that orphanage today because I wanted to understand you. So that I could make you happy.' He paused for a moment. 'I honestly had no idea of the effect it would have on me. I suppose that somewhere in the back of my mind I've always worried that being raised by parents like mine meant that I could never be a good parent myself.'

'You would make a wonderful father, Leo,' Dara said softly.

'I'm not so sure about *wonderful*. But after today I know I would like the opportunity to try.'

Dara looked up into her husband's eyes and saw the emotion there. 'Are you saying that you want us to start a family together?'

'We've been a family from the moment you agreed to spend the rest of your life as my wife. I want to take this next step with you—to start a new adventure.'

Dara closed her eyes, letting the air finally whoosh into her lungs. The fear of even daring to want this had stopped her from acknowledging her true feelings about Luca. Hearing Leo say these things… Hearing him shine a proverbial light on her deepest yearnings…

She looked up at her husband once more and saw that he was watching her quietly.

'I want to be Luca's mother.'

The words came out rushed and tumbled over each other on their way. But once she had said them out loud it was as though she truly understood herself for the first time. Her hands started to shake—a quake that continued up her arms and down into her abdomen.

Leo put his arms around her but she gently removed them, needing to pace for a moment with this newfound sense of terror coursing through her. It was one thing to be afraid of wanting something that she knew could never happen. But to admit that she wanted it…? To open herself to rejection and heartbreak…?

To Leo this was a new feeling—the idea of becoming a parent. But for Dara this was a sensation that had haunted her for years, a thought that had consumed her at times. She had fought back against the feelings of hopelessness by cutting the thought out of her life altogether and deciding that she no longer wanted to become a mother.

Now she knew the truth. She had never stopped wanting it. She had just been waiting for this moment.

'I can't believe this is happening...' Dara breathed, her thoughts swimming with the enormity of what they were discussing.

'It's only happening if you want it to.' Leo stood in front of her. 'I meant what I said on that beach three years ago. You will always be enough for me, Dara. You are more than I deserve.'

Dara felt the fear melt away as Leo's arms enveloped her, and all her worries seemed smaller all of a sudden. She breathed in the familiar scent of his aftershave and told herself that she needed to commit this perfect moment to memory.

'I want to start a family with you.' She pulled back to look into her husband's eyes. 'I want us to become Luca's parents. If he'll have us, that is.'

'Hearing him speak about you today, I have no doubt that he thinks just as much of you as you do of him,' Leo assured her.

'I hope so.' Dara bit her lip. 'Leo, once we take this step there is no going back. There will be no more impromptu trips to Paris—no more yachting for weeks along the Riviera. We'll have to consider school term times. It won't be just you and I.'

'I'm quite aware that children are a lot of responsibility.'

'I just want to make sure that you're certain this is what you want. That we aren't going into this with our eyes closed.'

'Dara, stop worrying and let yourself enjoy this. I have complete faith that you will plan every little detail perfectly. Just leave all the fun stuff to me.' He laughed.

Dara smiled. He was right—she was a ball of nerves. She took a deep breath, feeling a sense of excited anticipation hum through her veins.

'I will start proceedings in the morning.' Leo smiled. 'We can go to the orphanage ourselves.'

'I can hardly believe that this is happening.' Dara shook her head. 'Never in my wildest dreams...'

Leo pressed his lips tenderly to hers, his hands spanning her waist and pulling her to him in a tight embrace. 'I was afraid to share you with anyone else, but now I find myself wanting to show you off to the world. You amaze me with all you've overcome.'

'You're the one who helped me to overcome it.'

Their kiss turned from soft to heated, and the wind whipped around them as the sun dipped slowly towards the sea.

The next morning Dara arrived at the orphanage bright and early, with her husband by her side. They entered the common room just as the children had finished breakfast. No sooner had they stepped into the room than a tiny head of jet-black curls came barrelling towards them.

'Do you know the yo-yo man?'

Luca's eyes widened as he looked from Dara to Leo. Dara imagined her husband must look like a giant from the small boy's height, and yet he wasn't frightened.

'Luca, this is my husband Leo. He came here to meet you.'

The other children had filtered into the room, all their attention on the man with the yo-yo. Leo continued to delight the children with more tricks and Luca sat resolutely by his side, telling all the other children that 'the yo-yo man' had come to meet him.

Before they knew it, the children were called to have

lunch. As much as Dara wanted to stay there all day, she knew that now it was time for the official part of their visit.

As the lunch bell rang Luca's eyes turned wide and he ran to her. He looked up at her with that uncertain expression she had come to recognise so well after more than three months of visits.

'I promise that I will come back,' she said solemnly.

Luca was a child of abandonment, so he regularly made her promise that she was coming back in their same special way. Dara held out her pinkie finger, letting him lock it with his own tiny one.

She felt a hand at her waist. Leo stood by her side, watching the exchange with interest. 'Is this some secret handshake I don't know about?' he joked.

'I can teach it to you too,' Luca said quietly.

As Dara watched, her husband got down on his knees and promised the young boy that he would return. She felt a swell of love for this man who had helped her to overcome so much.

Leo straightened, and they waved as the boys ran in single file towards the lunchroom. Luca was the smallest of the lot.

'It was so good of you both to visit us today.' The friendly matron smiled as she welcomed them into her office. 'I couldn't help but notice your interest in little Luca,' she said speculatively.

Dara turned to the woman, meeting her gaze. 'My visits here haven't been as selfless as I've made them out to be.'

'You are a very kind woman, Dara. I don't believe that you came here out of your own interests.'

'Maybe not at first, but it has definitely become that way.'

'I have watched your progress with Luca intently. You know his history. He came to us a very scared and lonely boy. Since your visits he has changed. He talks more with the other children…he is more confident. Your attention did that for him.' She smiled again.

Leo stepped forward, taking Dara's trembling hand in his own. 'My wife and I would like to start proceedings to adopt Luca.' He felt the enormity of the words as he spoke them.

The other woman's eyes lit up with emotion and joy. 'Oh, after yesterday and today I confess that I had started to hope. But our hopes get dashed here far too often.'

'Our intentions are genuine. We would like to become Luca's parents,' Dara said. 'We know that the process is long, but we believe he will be happy with us. That we can give him a good home.'

Tears filled the old matron's eyes as she took one of Dara's hands in her own. 'You have no idea how long I've been waiting for you to realise that, Signora Valente.'

Dara stood by the fireplace, straightening the stockings and biting her lip. Was she jumping the gun by adding one smaller stocking beside their own two? She worried at her bottom lip for a moment, before making a final sweep of the living room. Piles of gifts lay stacked under the tree, ready to be torn open by eager little hands. She had wrapped each box painstakingly in bright paper with intricate bows. She wanted to make today as special as it could possibly be.

'Dara, stop worrying. The place looks amazing.' Leo strode into the living room, his hair lightly ruffled from being outside. 'You're going to have to get used to less organisation around here.'

'I know. I'm just keeping busy.' She sighed.

'He'll be here soon. You'll be kept *very* busy for the

weekend. Last chance… You're sure you don't want to hire a nanny?' He smiled mischievously.

'We will do just fine on our own.' Dara laughed as Leo swept her into his arms. 'He's just one little boy—how much work could he be?'

'I have feeling those are brave last words.'

She felt the excitement and the nerves coursing through him just as they did inside her. Leo pressed his mouth to hers softly, tracing the outline of her lips with own. She twined her fingers in the hair at the nape of his neck and sighed as he deepened the kiss, moulding his hands tightly to her waist. He shaped his body closely against hers, the warmth of him pressing hard against her.

She wanted to remember this moment for ever. Kissing the man she loved, here, in the home they had created, as they waited to welcome their son to his new home for the first time.

Their son.

In just a few moments she would officially be a mother. The realisation hit her like a freight train and she broke off their kiss just as the doorbell rang.

'Are you ready?'

Leo looked into her eyes, squeezing her hand tightly as they made their way to the entrance of the *castello*.

He smiled. 'I can't wait to see his face once he realises he's going to live in a real-life castle.'

Dara felt her nerves melt away as she saw the excited expression on Leo's face. Suddenly she just knew that everything was going to be wonderful from this moment on.

They opened the door to find their social worker helping Luca out of the car. His tiny face was turned up and he was looking at the *castello* with awe.

Dara ushered Luca inside, welcoming the social worker, who would be staying for the settling-in period. The adop-

tion process had definitely been speeded up by Leo, with
the Valente name seeming to cut through some of the
red tape, but it was far from over. This weekend was for
Luca—to ensure that he was happy to come and live with
them at the *castello* for good. They had a multitude of ac-
tivities planned and had put the finishing touches to his
bedroom.

Over the past weeks they had spent long hours bonding
with the young boy, going on day trips and meeting with
various officials. It was a gruelling process, but one that
was vital. Everyone had to be sure that he was happy to be
adopted by them. That was what mattered most.

Luca ran into the hall and barrelled into Leo's arms.
'Wow, you really *do* live in a castle!'

'I don't tell lies.' Leo smiled down at him.

'Will we be living here all the time?' he asked Dara in
a small voice.

Dara looked at the social worker, aware that her every
move was being assessed. 'If you would like it, this would
be our home, yes.' She turned to Leo, feeling her confidence begin to falter.

'Are there ghosts in this castle?' Luca asked suddenly.

'There used to be.' Leo looked pointedly at Dara for a
moment. 'But then a brave princess came and chased all
the ghosts away.'

Dara felt tiny fingers wrap around her own. She looked
down to see that Luca had grabbed on to her hand tightly
as they ascended the stairs to show him his new bedroom.
Her heart soared at this show of affection.

'I thought the knight was supposed to save the princess?' Dara questioned light-heartedly as she gripped her
son's hand.

'Sometimes the knight is the one who needs to be
saved.'

Leo caught her eye and Dara smiled to herself.

They had saved one another. Two broken souls who had somehow managed to make each other whole again. After all they had overcome in both their pasts, she was certain that the future could only be bright.

* * * * *

If you enjoyed Dara and Leo's story, you can find out where it all started in
RESISTING THE SICILIAN PLAYBOY
By Amanda Cinelli
available October 2015 wherever
Harlequin Presents books and ebooks are sold.
www.Harlequin.com

#3381 LARENZO'S CHRISTMAS BABY
One Night With Consequences
by Kate Hewitt
After two years behind bars, Larenzo Cavelli is determined to get his life back...starting with Emma Leighton. It was deception that imprisoned him, so what will happen when he discovers Emma's secret? One he might never be able to forgive...

#3382 BRAZILIAN'S NINE MONTHS' NOTICE
Hot Brazilian Nights!
by Susan Stephens
Chambermaid Emma Fane thinks her best friend's wedding will be the perfect distraction...until she spies Lucas Marcelos—father to her unborn child! It only took one night to change their lives, now they have nine months to face the consequences.

#3383 SHACKLED TO THE SHEIKH
Desert Brothers
by Trish Morey
Nanny Tora Burgess eagerly waits to meet her new boss—but is horrified to discover he's her red-hot, one-night lover! Rashid is cold, distant and has a shocking proposal that will shackle her to the sheikh forever!

#3384 BOUGHT FOR HER INNOCENCE
Greek Tycoons Tamed
by Tara Pammi
Jasmine Douglas is the only one who knows the darkness of Dmitri Karegas's past. But only Dmitri can help when she's forced to put her virginity up for sale. Now he must decide what to do with her...and her innocence!

REQUEST YOUR FREE BOOKS!

HARLEQUIN

Presents®

2 FREE NOVELS PLUS
2 FREE GIFTS!

YES! Please send me 2 FREE Harlequin Presents® novels and my 2 FREE gifts (gifts are worth about $10). After receiving them, if I don't wish to receive any more books, I can return the shipping statement marked "cancel." If I don't cancel, I will receive 6 brand-new novels every month and be billed just $4.30 per book in the U.S. or $5.24 per book in Canada. That's a saving of at least 13% off the cover price! It's quite a bargain! Shipping and handling is just 50¢ per book in the U.S. and 75¢ per book in Canada.* I understand that accepting the 2 free books and gifts places me under no obligation to buy anything. I can always return a shipment and cancel at any time. Even if I never buy another book, the two free books and gifts are mine to keep forever.

106/306 HDN GHRP

Name _____ (PLEASE PRINT)

Address _____ Apt. #

City _____ State/Prov. _____ Zip/Postal Code

Signature (if under 18, a parent or guardian must sign)

Mail to the **Reader Service:**
IN U.S.A.: P.O. Box 1867, Buffalo, NY 14240-1867
IN CANADA: P.O. Box 609, Fort Erie, Ontario L2A 5X3

**Are you a current subscriber to Harlequin Presents® books
and want to receive the larger-print edition?
Call 1-800-873-8635 or visit www.ReaderService.com.**

* Terms and prices subject to change without notice. Prices do not include applicable taxes. Sales tax applicable in N.Y. Canadian residents will be charged applicable taxes. Offer not valid in Quebec. This offer is limited to one order per household. Not valid for current subscribers to Harlequin Presents books. All orders subject to credit approval. Credit or debit balances in a customer's account(s) may be offset by any other outstanding balance owed by or to the customer. Please allow 4 to 6 weeks for delivery. Offer available while quantities last.

Your Privacy—The Reader Service is committed to protecting your privacy. Our Privacy Policy is available online at www.ReaderService.com or upon request from the Reader Service.

We make a portion of our mailing list available to reputable third parties that offer products we believe may interest you. If you prefer that we not exchange your name with third parties, or if you wish to clarify or modify your communication preferences, please visit us at www.ReaderService.com/consumerschoice or write to us at Reader Service Preference Service, P.O. Box 9062, Buffalo, NY 14240-9062. Include your complete name and address.

HPI5

SPECIAL EXCERPT FROM

◆ HARLEQUIN

Presents.

*Playboy Prince Andres of Petras is bound by royal
duty and must finally pay the price for his past
sins—by marrying the lost princess of Tirimia. From
fiery passion to sinfully seductive kisses, is this one
Christmas gift the prince will be keeping...forever?*

*Read on for a sneak preview of
A CHRISTMAS VOW OF SEDUCTION,
the first book in* **PRINCES OF PETRAS**,
the sensational new duet by
USA TODAY *bestselling author* **Maisey Yates**.

She looked down, caught the glitter of her engagement
ring on the hand that was squeezing him. Then she looked
back up at his face. A mistake.

She barely had a chance to register the hot, angry glitter in his dark eyes before he closed the distance between
them, his mouth crashing down onto hers.

The force of him pushing her back against the wall
crushed their bodies together as he angled his head and
slipped his tongue between her lips.

He proved then what he'd said before. He had the
power. She could do nothing, not in this moment. Nothing but simply surrender to the heat coursing through her,
to the electrical current crackling over her skin with a
kind of intensity she'd never even imagined existed.

His hands were firm and sure on her hips, his body
pressing her to the wall as he sought restitution for her
attempt at claiming control.

"You want a fight?" He growled the words against her mouth. "I can give you a fight, Princess. We don't have to do this the easy way." He angled his head, parting his lips from hers, kissing her neck. She shivered, fear and arousal warring for pride of place inside her. "But if you want to test me, you have to be prepared for the results. I do not know what manner of man you have been exposed to in the past, but I am not one that can be easily manipulated."

He rocked his hips against hers, showing her full evidence of the effect she was having on his body. She had spent so much of her life being ignored that eliciting such a powerful response from such a man gratified her in ways she never could have anticipated.

She didn't know a kiss could be so many different things. That it could serve so many purposes. That it could make her feel hot, cold, afraid, enraptured. But it did. It was everything, and nothing she should ever have allowed to happen between them.

Don't miss
A CHRISTMAS VOW OF SEDUCTION
by USA TODAY *bestselling author Maisey Yates,*
available November 2015 wherever
Harlequin Presents® books and ebooks are sold.

www.Harlequin.com

HPEXP1015

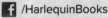